"What does my lady prefer [...]
asked as he flipped his hand [...]
gestured to t[...]

[...] he was wanna Fucking White.

I stared at the cornucopia of choices stacked and hung in the back of the van.

"Well, the scythe is always fun," I mused. "But unwieldy in tight places like Jimmy always calls us to. Same thing with the chainsaw, and it stalled the last time I used it in Mesa Verde, which was almost very bad."

David flinched at the memory. "True. How about an axe?"

I tilted my head as I examined the gleaming blade of my favorite axe. "No, not today. Just not in the mood for that, or the sword."

Dave's eyes lit up. "Wait. I know what you want."

I gave him a look as he took off around to the driver's side back door of the van. In a second, he was back and he was brandishing the most beautiful thing I've ever seen in my life.

"I call it the home-run-you-through," he said as he held out a heavy wooden baseball bat that had a long, wicked sharp spearhead firmly attached to the end by some kind of metal twine. "And I'm copyrighting that as soon as we find a patent office, so no trying to rip me off."

I grinned as I reached out to take the bat. It was balanced perfectly and would do the job of both smashing and stabbing zombie heads nicely.

"You *do* know what to get a girl for Christmas," I murmured as I put my handgun back in my waistband and stepped back to perfor[...]

BY JESSE PETERSEN

LIVING WITH THE DEAD

Married with Zombies
Flip this Zombie

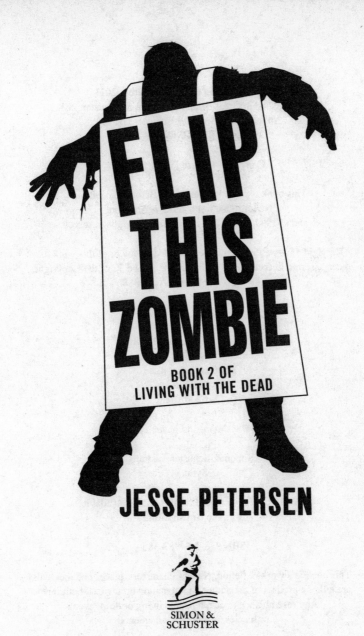

FLIP THIS ZOMBIE

BOOK 2 OF
LIVING WITH THE DEAD

JESSE PETERSEN

SIMON &
SCHUSTER

London · New York · Sydney · Toronto

A CBS COMPANY

First published in the USA by Orbit, 2011
First published in Great Britain by Simon & Schuster, 2011
An imprint of Simon & Schuster UK Ltd
A CBS COMPANY

Copyright © Jesse Petersen, 2011

The right of Jesse Petersen to be identified as author of this work has
been asserted in accordance with sections 77 and 78 of the Copyright,
Designs and Patents Act, 1988.

1 3 5 7 9 10 8 6 4 2

Simon & Schuster UK Ltd
1st Floor
222 Gray's Inn Road
London
WC1X 8HB

www.simonandschuster.co.uk

Simon & Schuster Australia
Sydney

A CIP catalogue record for this book is available
from the British Library

ISBN 978-1-84983-386-8

Printed in the UK by CPI Cox & Wyman, Reading RGI 8EX

For Michael

FLIP
THIS
ZOMBIE

CHAPTER 1

Do what you love and the zombies will follow.

When the zombie plague struck, I was just an office schlub. You know the type. I was a coffee-fetching, doing-the-work-and-getting-no-credit, screamed-at-by-suits kind of girl who hated every damn second of her dead-end job. Well, I still have a dead-end job...*undead* end, I guess is more accurate. But instead of working for the man, I work for myself. So I guess the lesson is that if you find work that's meaningful, that you love, you can start your own business and make it successful.

So what's my job?

Zombiebusters Extermination, Inc at your service.

My husband David suggested we add the "Inc" to make it seem more professional. I guess in the old days we would have had a website and all that, too, but now none of that exists anymore, at least not in the badlands where the zombies still roam free.

I have to say, I liked being in business for myself and I liked working with my husband as my partner. The zombie apocalypse had been surprisingly good for our marriage (sounds weird, I know, but it's true) and since we escaped Seattle a few months before, we'd been doing great.

But that isn't to say the whole "not working for the man" thing didn't have its disadvantages. Which is something we were discussing as we drove down a lonely stretch of dusty highway in Arizona. Why Arizona? Well, it was November and fucking freezing anywhere else. So we did what old people had been doing for generations and snowbirded our asses down South. I figured when the weather got better up North, we'd decide what to do next.

"Why did we take another job from Jimmy?" Dave asked with annoyance lacing his voice.

I looked up from the business book I was reading. We'd looted it and about twenty more from a bookstore a few weeks back. I was all about making this work, you see. Someday, I would be the Donald Trump or Bill Gates of zombie killing. Only with better hair, obviously.

"Um, we took a job from Jimmy because he pays," I said.

Dave shot me a side glance that was filled with incredulity. "Not well. Last time I think he gave us a six-pack and we killed three zombies for his chicken-ass."

I laughed. "Hey, that's two brews per zombie. Anyway, he trades with everyone and brings us new business at least once a week. He may not pay us as well as … well … anyone else, but think of it as brand building."

"My ass." Dave didn't even smile. "He has a lot of shit stockpiled in his basement, I know he does. This time before we start, we should tell that asshole we want payment up front. Medical supplies and some canned goods."

I tossed my book in the back of the van.

Oh, didn't I mention it? We drive a van. Dave likes to call it the Mystery Machine because it's totally circa 1975, but it runs like a gem and is heavy enough to do some push work when needed. Plus, I had *way* too much fun painting "Zombiebusters Exterminators, Inc" on the side and "Who Ya Gonna Call?" on the back.

That one always gets a chuckle since there's no way to call anyone anymore. If people want us, they have to post notes in the survivor camps and we go looking for them. Trust me, sometimes by the time we've gotten to a job, there hasn't been anyone left to pay us. I always feel kind of badly about that, but seriously, if you haven't figured out how to protect yourself after three months of zombie hell . . . well, you sort of deserve what you get.

"Look, you're the muscle in this operation," I said as I settled back in my seat and slung my booted feet onto the dash. As I flicked a little piece of brains left over after our last job from the toe, I continued, "If you want to strong-arm the guy up front, be my guest."

We were approaching our destination now and Dave slowly maneuvered the vehicle off the highway into the area of what was once southern Phoenix. There were signs of zombie activity everywhere here, both from the initial outbreak in the city and more recently. Black sludge pooled in the gutters and blood streaked the walls of buildings. It was all so commonplace to us, we didn't really see it anymore. Nor did we flinch when a single zombie stepped into a crosswalk ahead of us.

He lurched forward, his right hand missing and his

arm on the same side waving in a disconnected way as he moved. He had fresh blood on his chin and he grunted and groaned loudly enough that we could hear him even with the windows partly up.

We watched him make his slow cross for a bit, both of us staring with bored disinterest. Then Dave gunned the engine.

The sound made the zombie turn and he stared at us with his blank, dead, red eyes that never quite focused. Still, he seemed to recognize the potential for food on some primal level and he let out a roar.

Dave floored the van at the same time the zombie started a half-assed jog toward us. We collided mid-intersection and the zombie, gooey and rotting, took the brunt of the impact. His skin split, sending gore and guts flying from the seams of his torn clothing to splatter on our hood and the ground around the van. He lay half-wrapped around our bumper, staring up at us as he squealed and clawed along the metal of the hood like he could somehow hoist himself up and get to us, even though his lower body was probably gone.

"Want me to take care of that?" I asked as I reached in the back for an axe.

"No way," Dave said. "And let you get ahead on Death Count?"

I laughed as he changed gears and rolled back in reverse. The zombie fell backward and disappeared from view until my husband got far enough away. Sure enough, his lower half was gone, split off from the initial impact of the "accident."

Dave lined up the wheel of the van and rolled forward again. He didn't stop until we felt the satisfying rock of hitting the zombie skull and popping it like a melon.

Once that was done, Dave put the van in neutral. He pulled his knife from his waistband and carefully etched a new hash mark on the steering wheel, which was already covered in crevices and digs from previous kills. Pretty soon we were going to have to move on to the door.

"That's another one for the Mystery Machine." When I laughed, he looked at me. "So if I'm the muscle of the operation," he said, returning to our earlier conversation, "what does that make you?"

"Silly," I laughed. "I'm the braaaaains, of course. And the beauty."

I fluffed my hair as he threw the van in first and we roared toward our first job of the week.

Fire-bombing had been the way our government had dealt with the zombie plague. Whole cities wiped out without warning and without waiting to see if there were survivors as the military kept its troops in the air rather than on the ground, where they could become undead soldiers.

Phoenix hadn't escaped this "final solution" mentality any more than Seattle or L.A. or San Diego had. While some parts in the south end of the city were still partially intact, the downtown area itself was a mass of twisted burned metal and half walls.

Despite that, downtown was where Jimmy No-Toes lived. Why No-Toes? Other than that he had no toes on his left foot, I have no fucking idea.

"Watch yourself," David muttered as he cut the

van's engine and looked at the burned-out building our "employer" for the day called home.

It had once been a barber shop, I guess, and Jimmy had found it hilarious to paint the old-fashioned barber's pole with black blood and sludge from dead zombies. Most of whom *we* had killed, by the way.

I pulled my pistol from the back of my waistband as I opened up the passenger door and both of us checked around us. Guns were a great way to dispose of zombies, but the sound brought others running to check it out, so whenever possible we used other tools.

David pulled open the back of the van and I looked inside at our arsenal, collected over the past few months and tested tried and true (seriously, we should have made a stamp for these things that said SARAH AND DAVID APPROVED! Maybe next apocalypse, huh?).

"What does my lady prefer for today?" Dave asked as he flipped his hand palm side up and gestured to the weaponry before me like he was Vanna Fucking White.

I stared at the cornucopia of choices stacked and hung in the back of the van.

"Well, the scythe is always fun," I mused. "But unwieldy in tight places like Jimmy always calls us to. Same thing with the chainsaw, and it stalled the last time I used it in Mesa Verde, which was almost very bad."

David flinched at the memory. "True. How about an axe?"

I tilted my head as I examined the gleaming blade of my favorite axe. "No, not today. Just not in the mood for that, or the sword."

Dave's eyes lit up. "Wait. I know what you want."

I gave him a look as he took off around to the driver's

side back door of the van. In a second, he was back and he was brandishing the most beautiful thing I've ever seen in my life.

"I call it the home-run-you-through," he said as he held out a heavy wooden baseball bat that had a long, wicked sharp spearhead firmly attached to the end by some kind of metal twine. "And I'm copyrighting that as soon as we find a patent office, so no trying to rip me off."

I grinned as I reached out to take the bat. It was balanced perfectly and would do the job of both smashing and stabbing zombie heads nicely.

"You *do* know what to get a girl for Christmas," I murmured as I put my handgun back in my waistband and stepped back to perform a few practice swings and stabs in the air.

"Oh no, baby," Dave said as he grabbed a machete and shoved his shotgun into the sling around his back. "This isn't half as cool as what I have planned for our first zombie Christmas."

I laughed, but the sound faded as he shut the double back doors of the van and we faced Jimmy's barber shop. "Want to do this?"

Dave nodded and we inched forward, ever at the ready. The door to the shop was locked, but the glass around it had been broken, rendering the lock useless anyway, even to a really stupid zombie. Dave rolled his eyes and reached through to throw the latch and let us in.

Jimmy had no toes, but I should also mention he wasn't exactly brainy, either. Probably why he was constantly asking for our help. He could find a pod of zombies better than anyone I've ever met, but he was too lazy or dimwitted or *both* to do anything about it.

"Jimmy?" David called out into the dusty dark of the front room of the barbershop. "Hey, it's ZBE, Inc!"

I rolled my eyes. "God damn it," I whispered. "That isn't what we call ourselves."

He never looked at me, just kept moving forward. "It's a perfectly legitimate shortening of our name and I think it's catchy."

"We have a fucking brand to maintain here, David," I insisted. "All the marketing books say—"

I didn't finish because off to my right I heard a faint scrape. Both of us spun toward it, weapons lifted.

"Fucking Jimmy, if that's you come out or you'll be shish kabob in about three seconds," I snapped.

There was a low, entirely unzombie-like chuckle and then Jimmy himself stood up from behind a bank of barber chairs. He had long, unkempt hair and I could smell him from across the room. And it isn't like anyone could take a long, hot, fabulous, steamy shower with shower gel and shampoo and conditioner that smelled like lilac and...oh, sorry, had a moment of fantasy there...but most of us had figured out how to freshen up in the worst of circumstances.

Not Jimmy, though I doubted he'd been much of a hygiene freak even when the world was normal.

"Nothing turns me on more than hearing you two bicker. How's the make-up sex?" he said with a laugh.

I wrinkled my nose. "You are the most disgusting human being I've ever met."

He bowed slightly, greasy hair falling over his face for a moment and blocking out the crooked, dirty teeth and the scraggly beard that completed the picture.

"Pleased for the compliment."

"Asshole," David muttered.

Jimmy laughed again, finishing it up with a wet, sickly cough that made me frown. As much as I disliked the guy, the fact that he always sounded like he was on the edge of keeling over worried me. There weren't many of us humans left in the badlands, we had to do everything we could to stay alive.

"So what do you need, No-Toes?" I asked with a sigh. "We saw your note in the Sun Devil camp. It said something about a pod?"

The jovial quality to Jimmy's dirty face faded and his bloodshot eyes went wide and, to my surprise, filled with fear. His hands shook as he gripped the back of one of the barber's chairs.

"Y-Yeah, but this ain't no ordinary pod, Sarah," he said with a shake of his head. "There's something different."

"Different?" David said with an incredulous lift of his eyebrows. "What the hell do you mean, *different*? Zombies are already pretty *different*."

Jimmy shook his head quickly. "But these are . . . bigger. And faster."

"Jimmy," Dave sighed in exasperation. "What the fuck have you been drinkin', man?"

"Naw, it's not that," Jimmy insisted as he came out from behind the chairs and hurried toward my husband with outreached hands. Both of us flinched at the increased stench in the air that wafted ahead of him. "I swear, dude. These ones, when they look at you . . . it's like they *see* you."

"Uh-huh."

Dave shot me a look that said he thought Jimmy was cuckoo for Cocoa Puffs, but I wasn't so sure. He looked genuinely afraid and not in the normal "I saw a zombie and I'm too lazy to kill it myself" way.

"So where did you see these...these...*bionic* zombies?" I asked.

Jimmy turned on me, his neck craning as he jerked out a quick series of nods. "Yeah, bionic. That's right!"

"Where did you see them?" I repeated softly.

"Near that church by where the convention center used to be downtown," he muttered and then let out a shiver.

I nodded. The governmental bombing had destroyed most of the buildings in the main downtown area, but the church, which was actually called St. Mary's Basilica, had remained standing. Religious nuts called it a sign and kept trying to go there to pray or whatever, which of course brought the zombies there in droves to feed. They might as well have changed the name to St. Mary's Feed Trough and started taking reservations from the zombie horde.

Would they require a jacket and tie for that?

I sighed. "Okay, we'll check it out."

Dave shot me a look, but my expression kept him from saying anything to me. He shook his head. "Yeah, but we're going to need to get *paid* this time."

All Jimmy's fear fled his face and he looked at Dave like he was the picture of innocence. He had the gall to sound affronted when he said, "Of course. I *always* pay."

"Six beers for three zombies is *not* a fair trade fucking system, No-Toes," Dave barked. "We get paid in food, medical supplies, ammo, all kinds of shit by everyone else but you."

I couldn't help but smile. Yeah, my baby was an ass-kicker. Gotta love that in a guy. Jimmy didn't seem to, though. His face darkened with fear again and just a touch of anger.

"I don't got nothing else," he insisted.

Dave moved forward. "Look, you little looting scum, I know you keep finding pods because you're hauling all over gathering up shit to trade at the survivor camps. You can't say anything that's going to make me believe otherwise. And this time I want payment up front or no killy the zombies, bud."

Jimmy shot me a look as if he hoped I might take his side in all this, but I just shrugged as I flicked a piece of lint off the blade at the end of my baseball bat. Finally his shoulders slumped.

"*Fine*," he said. "I'll go get you some shit now and I'll give you some more when you come back with zombie heads."

Dave smiled, ignoring Jimmy's muttering of all kinds of slurs as he turned on his heel and headed toward the doors that led to the basement area where he kept his stash.

"Nice," I muttered when he was out of earshot. "Very brawn, not brains of you."

"He's finally fucking cracked," Dave said with a shake of his head. He paced around the cramped barber shop restlessly. "Bionic zombies? And thank you, by the way, for encouraging him with that little label."

"You saw his face, though," I said as I stared where our little friend had disappeared. "I think he's genuinely scared."

"No way." Dave shook his head. "He's probably just high. Or drunk. Or both."

"He certainly reeks of it, but I don't think so," I said. "Whatever he saw, he believes it's real. Are we going to check it out?"

Dave chuckled as we heard Jimmy coming back in the distance. "Of course we're going to fucking check it out. We're the Zombiebusters, aren't we?"

CHAPTER 2

The question: what color is my parachute?
The answer: blood red, brains gray, sludge black.

We ended up with quite a haul as pre-payment for the bionic zombie job. Two large first aid kits with actual antibiotic ointment (quite the coup because infection took down as many survivors as zombies did by this point) and a three-pack of Ramen.

Doesn't sound like much to you? Well, sit there in your non-zombie paradise and judge then. Trust me, that shit was worth its weight in gold and then some in the badlands.

But neither of us was thinking about our good fortune as we slowly pulled around a few burned-out vehicles and maneuvered past a portion of a once-four-star hotel that had collapsed months ago.

No, when we pulled into the Basilica's half-empty parking lot, I think both of us were pondering the idea of a bionic zombie. A zombie with powers. Superpowers.

Well, at least with a little more awareness.

David shut the van down and both of us looked up at

the imposing building. On some level, I sort of understood why idiot "pilgrims" would keep coming here despite the danger and even almost certain death (or living death).

Every other building on this block had been flattened, so with all that destruction around it, the old-fashioned mission-style building *did* stand out like a beacon. The only signs that anything within its walls had changed were the burned-out cars in the parking lot and the streaked blood that stained the stucco walls on all four sides and from the base of the building to about six or seven feet high (about as high as a person could reach).

Of course, *inside* was a whole different matter.

"I hate this place," I muttered as we got out of the van and went around the back to load up on weapons.

Unlike at Jimmy's hideout when we'd been lightly armed, this time we each took multiple weapons and grabbed for plenty of extra ammo, plus a big burlap bag for zombie heads. We'd been around this block a few times, we knew to be ready.

"Well, you were always more of an agnostic," David said as we moved through the dusty parking lot.

The front doors of the Basilica were the same material as the stucco walls, meant to blend into them almost seamlessly. The bloody handprints that stained the walls also covered the door and were heaviest all around the handle. I wrinkled my nose with disgust as I shoved my hand into my sleeve and pushed the door open without touching it.

"Still fastidious after all these months," David muttered.

"I. Don't. Like. Goo."

I shot him a glare when he dared to *laugh* at my suffering, but quickly refocused on matters at hand.

There was a small foyer area directly behind the doors and it flooded with light from outside for a brief moment before those same doors swung shut behind us. In that brightness I saw a bulletin board that had once touted church socials and announcements but was now tacked full with multiple layers of handwritten prayers and desperate pleas for news of lost loved ones.

There was also a blank space where a collection box once sat. Half the note requesting funds from visitors and parishioners alike was rotting away on the wall behind the space. That box had been ripped free early in the outbreak, when people still thought money had value.

Times had certainly changed. We used Benjamins as fire starters now.

Once our eyes adjusted to the darkness, we moved into the main church area with extra caution because the area was so exposed and open.

The pews that had once been so carefully arranged to face the front of the church for weddings or sermons were now overturned, broken, and in some cases, even burned. The high domed ceiling rose up above us and the stained glass that capped it sent sprays of color down across the marble floors.

Red was the main color in the dim hall, red from the glass, the red of the torn carpet that had once lined the main aisle...red from the blood.

Over the past few months I'd developed an abiding hatred for red. Too bad, really. It had always been my color.

"Anybody home?" Dave called out.

We waited for a moment to see what the call brought us. Often any loud sound brings zombies coming to check out the new food source. That was why it was better not to use guns in close quarters or to shout too loudly during a fight, because that was like setting off a "zombie goodies" beacon.

But today Dave's question brought nothing but silence in return.

"I don't see or hear any pilgrims, either. Maybe the morons finally figured out this wasn't an oasis," I said softly. "Stopped making themselves zombie bait."

"I doubt it," he said with a sigh. "Some people *never* stop making themselves zombie bait. That's why we have a job, remember?"

I was about to come up with some kind of witty reply when there was a crash across the large hall. Both of us lifted our weapons higher as we peered through the hazy light. At some point, someone had the sense to build a sort of bunker on the elevated platform that held the altar and the sound had come from there.

"Here we come, bionic zombies," I muttered.

Now when all this started, I was a normal person. Okay, a *reasonably* normal person. The first zombies I killed scared the shit out of me. I dreamed of them, my sleep troubled by nightmares where I was overrun, overcome, bitten and changed just like so many people I knew and loved had been. I saw them in every dark corner when I was awake, too. For at least the first month, everything made me jump.

But over time, fear had given way to anger and my kills had gotten easier and bloodier. And then anger gave way to pure and simple job satisfaction. I mean, when I looked at a dead zombie head on a spike, I thought, "Hey, *I* did that. Picasso would be proud. Especially how I rearranged that eye."

In short, I was a proficient zombie warrior and took pride in my work, but that first thrill of emotion was now gone.

Except for today. Now, with the idea of a newer, scarier kind of zombie out there for me to kill, my heart raced and my bat shook just a little.

If Dave noticed my new attitude, he didn't say anything. As we reached the altar, he merely motioned his head to the left and then to the right, indicating we should each take a side and come around the back to see what had caused the crash. I chose to go to the right and we reached the sides of the bunker at about the same time. Peering over the low wall, I suppressed a sigh.

There was a zombie down in the bunker all right, munching happily over the corpse of a woman. The victim was unkempt, her dress ragged and dirty. The only nice thing about her was the huge diamond-encrusted cross that hung from her obviously broken neck. A pilgrim, no doubt, come here to find God like the rest. Instead she had found this.

Her eyes were blank and dead for now, but that would soon change as the zombie ate at her freshly killed flesh and sucked at the blood that trickled from the ripped and tattered wound at her chest.

Her killer was wearing the tattered remains of a police uniform, complete with shiny, black baton that still hung from his nearly shredded belt. I eyed it with interest because it would make a great bludgeon for our purposes now that he didn't need it anymore.

Dave took the lead. He vaulted over the bunker like a cat and, with a slash of his machete, took the head of the cop zombie just as it lifted its red eyes and recognized there was a new person to kill. In another hacking motion, Dave beheaded the victim of the zombie.

"Nothing bionic about this one," he said as he grabbed the zombie cop's skull by the unkempt, once-blond hair and lifted it up. The dead flesh of its scalp strained and cracked as Dave held it up to the light so we could see it better. "Just a regular, stupid zombie."

"Yeah, well get its regular, stupid baton, then," I said with a nod, but before I could say anything more, three additional zombies appeared from the doorway that led to the back of the church behind Dave.

"Oh, and correction. There are *several* regular, stupid zombies," I said as I hurried around the bunker to face our enemy.

You know that one move every girl lead makes in kung fu or horror movies? The one where she's wearing head-to-toe black leather and she has a kicky haircut and she crouches down on one knee with her opposite foot sort of laid out and then she slices and dices...all while looking super doable?

Well, the Kate Beckinsales and urban fantasy heroines of the world lied to us. That does *not* work. First, leather is hot, it stinks to high heaven, and it limits your movement. Oh, and it chafes like a motherfucker.

Second, you just don't want to get lower than your prey and you certainly don't want to be all off-balance. That's a great way to go down on your ass and have a rabid zombie on top of you.

How do I know this? Well, I've tried some stuff since the outbreak, okay? Might as well learn from my mistakes.

Anyway, instead of making the pretty movie move,

I jumped down from the elevated altar with a cry and smashed the baseball bat down on the crown of the first zombie's skull. There was a wet, satisfying thud as his rotting head disintegrated and he fell at my feet.

With a tug, I freed my bat from his broken brains and turned on another, which was lurching toward me. His torn and bloody priest vestments flopped around his arms and the wooden rosary around his neck swung as if he were directing a rather passionate sermon. I set my legs and raised my bat over one shoulder.

"Sarah steps up to the base, Sarah swings and..."

I hurled the bat around and cracked the zombie straight in the temple. He gave a pained and faint growl as he staggered backward, bounced off the wall (leaving a trail of sludge behind him), and fell to the ground where he lay still and silent.

"Home run!" I said, lifting my arms in victory as I turned to find David finishing off the third and final zombie with a swinging thwack of his machete. "The crowd goes wild!"

"It was a foul," he corrected as he gathered up the head of the zombie he had felled and tossed it in the sack with the others.

So you're probably wondering why take the heads. Well, about a month before, Jimmy No-Toes and some of the other "clients" who frequented our extermination service had gotten really weird about wanting to verify our kills. So we started bringing the heads back in order to collect our full payment for the jobs we did. I hadn't developed the stomach for head removal and collection, though, so that fell to my husband.

I wrinkled my nose as David moved to take the heads of

the two zombies I'd killed. I turned my face so I wouldn't see him hack and muttered, "Foul my ass."

He arched a brow at me as he tied off the sack and flung it over his shoulder like a really screwed up Santa Claus. You did *not* want this guy coming to your house Christmas Eve, that's for sure.

"You *really* want to argue with the ump?" he laughed. "That's how you get thrown out of a game. Now, why don't we clear the rest of the building?"

I shrugged as I folded my arms with what I admit was a bit of a childish pout. "What's the point? There are no bionic zombies."

"Did you really think there were?" Dave asked as he shot me a look from the corner of his eye.

I shrugged. "I don't know. Jimmy seemed so...so... *honest* about being afraid of whatever he saw here. There are a lot of ways you could describe that guy, but honest isn't normally one of them. I guess it just caught my attention."

"I still say he was drunk...or stoned," Dave said with a shrug as he motioned me deeper into the church. "Actually, I'm going to ask him to pay us the second half of his debt with whatever he's been smoking. Sounds fun."

For the next twenty minutes we didn't talk much as we cleared the rest of the big building. There wasn't anything else to be found, though. As we returned to the van and reloaded our stuff, I shook my head.

"It's never been that empty," I mused as I stared up at the pristine building amidst collapsed and ruined hell.

Dave nodded. "Yeah. Normally we find a couple of lurkers and a half-dead pilgrim per trip."

"It's kind of creepy," I whispered.

He patted my arm as we finished loading up. "Well, maybe you're right. Maybe the pilgrims have finally gotten the message that it isn't safe. If they stopped coming here, the zombies would have to find somewhere else to go for their buffet."

I continued to stare at the building even as I climbed into the van for the return trip to Jimmy's hideout. "*Maybe*. I mean, I hope so. But there's something just so *off* about it."

Dave turned in his seat to face me. "Come on, Sarah, you aren't letting yourself get all caught up in Jimmy's ghost... er, *zombie* story, are you?"

I shrugged. "Why can't it be possible that there are different kinds of zombies? That maybe there *are* ones who are stronger?"

"Because the zombies were made by people and those people are all long gone. Those... those *creatures* are just lumps of empty flesh that can't... *die* like they're supposed to. They don't evolve or think or feel, they just feed. You know that." He turned the key and the engine roared to life. "Or at least you should after all this time."

I frowned as I stared out the window in silence. Part of me knew that Dave was right. That I was just letting myself get worked up by a drunk with a vivid imagination.

But part of me still wondered, as we turned away from the church and crossed over the shambled tracks of what used to be the Metro, if what No-Toes said about bionics was possible.

And what would happen if it was.

CHAPTER 3

Who moved my cheese? And my shotgun?

When we pulled back up to Jimmy's barbershop a short while later, things were almost back to normal. Or... whatever the closest thing was in the zombieverse. I won't say I was totally convinced that the bionics didn't exist, but I was well on my way to putting them out of my mind.

"Want to wait here?" Dave asked as he put the pistol he'd rested on the dashboard back into his waistband and reached in the back for the burlap sack of heads.

I shrugged. "I guess I can start thinking about food while you make the drop."

Now normally we didn't split up, but David was armed and this was merely a swap job with Jimmy. In and out.

Still, I put my own 9mm in reach on the dash as David exited the vehicle. As he walked up to the shop door, the bag of heads swung at his side in rhythm to his step and dripped sludge behind him like a surreal telling of Hansel and Gretel (I guess that would make Jimmy the witch and would explain why he was dressing the part).

When Dave disappeared into the shop, I reached behind me and grabbed an old tin box we'd taken from a military surplus store we'd found a while back. When I opened it, I groaned.

Within lay the food of champions. And that wasn't saying much. Some old PowerBars (and not even in the good flavors) stared back at me. There was a bit of beef jerky and a couple of MRE rations.

God damn, I missed food. *Real* food.

Not fast food, really. I'd stopped craving pizza and burgers and fries within the first few weeks and my body had thanked me for it by leaning out. No, now I missed weird stuff. Like cereal with skim milk. Or yogurt.

I know, I know, here I was in the middle of the desert and I was longing for bacteria-laden dairy. Whatever. I still wanted it. That's just how the brain works, I guess.

After much consideration, I chose to pull out the bag of jerky and tossed it on the driver's seat while I put the rest of the tin back in place behind us. We couldn't eat much from our meager collection, not until we scrounged up some more stock to replace it, which meant either making a few store runs for trade items or taking a job from one of our better-paying customers.

When I glanced toward the barber shop, I saw Dave coming back out. He no longer carried the burlap sack of heads, but he had another curiously *small* paper bag in his hand, a remnant of the fast food I no longer craved.

He threw open the driver's side door and got in. His lips pursed and he yanked the jerky bag from under his ass and tossed it and the take-out sack into my lap.

"What?" I asked as he roared the engine almost to the point of flooding it and gunned it back toward the highway.

He didn't answer, but his white knuckles told a pretty fucking clear story.

"What?" I repeated. "What did Jimmy say?"

"Wasn't there," David's teeth never unclenched as he spoke. "Left a note saying to leave the heads by the door."

"Ah." I looked down at the bag in my lap. "I assume *this* is what he left for payment?"

Dave blinked. "Oh yes. Please, open it!"

I sighed as I unrolled the greasy bag and reached inside. I pulled out one small box decorated with cartoon characters.

"Bandages," I said as I stared at the colorful artwork.

"Oh no," Dave said, enunciating very carefully now. "Not just bandages. Sponge-Fucking-Bob-Square-Damn-Pants bandages."

"He lives in a pineapple under the…" I trailed off as Dave's eye twitched. "Sorry." I shook the box. "Half-full."

David jolted his head toward me. "You're kidding."

"Nope." I put the box back in its bag and tossed it in the back for storage later.

There was no response from my husband for probably about five miles.

"Fucking cheapskate," Dave finally muttered, his knuckles white on the steering wheel as he stared at the expanse of highway.

I didn't answer, mostly because there was nothing to say. I mean, we'd have cheerfully dressed wounds for a little bit, but I doubted Dave wanted to hear that.

I stared out my window. We hardly even noticed the burned and bloody cars that had been cleared to either

side of the road anymore. They were just part of the landscape now, like the desert or the mountains.

There was only barren wasteland to our left and right.
Once it had been part of a city, but now...nothing. Well,
almost nothing. Off in the distance, I saw movement down
on the streets and in the flattened parks. Zombies lurching
around, looking to feed.

"Hey, slow down," I said as I reached in the back for
one of the rifles with a scope. "I think some target practice
might do me good."

Dave did as I'd asked, dropping our speed gradually
until we were only going about ten miles an hour. I rolled
down the window and balanced my gun on the ledge.
Carefully I took aim at a zombie dressed in filthy doctor's
scrubs who was standing on a street corner by what was
left of a bus stop. Just standing there, like he was waiting
for the 5:30 to...*hell*, I guess.

I gently squeezed the trigger and was rewarded by the
plume of blood that burst from the back of his head. He
collapsed in a heap on the sidewalk. I kept my eye focused
through the sight of the rifle and watched as, sure enough,
the explosive sound of the gunfire echoing in the desert
air brought zombies racing from the rubble in a wave of
snarling, drooling, sludge-vomiting unison.

"They're coming for the on-ramp," I said mildly as I
pulled off another shot and dropped not one, but two when
the bullet pierced rotting flesh so easily that it maintained
its velocity and killing power.

"Ten points for two," Dave said without acknowledging my first statement. He was starting to sound less
pissed now, as he always did when the killing started. We

were a bloodthirsty little pair. What can I say? That MTV
Generation thing might have had some validity.

David kept the car barely rolling even as the mob of
zombies panted and weaved their way up the off-ramp.
On- and off-ramps, especially ones with steeper grades,
always trip zombies up, sometimes literally. They just
don't have the mind power to figure them out, so it's hilarious. Like watching really stupid chickens peck around in
a fucked-up coop.

Eventually, though, a hefty portion of the zombies
I'd stirred up managed to make it up the hill and rolled
toward us in an undead wave of arms (and lack of arms)
and unkempt insanity.

I fired off a couple more shots, this time faster since the
zombie horde was closer than ever.

"Any time now, sweetheart," I said as I reloaded and
fired a few more rounds.

"Oh." Dave said, as if he'd been distracted and forgotten he had the power to save our asses. "Sure."

He geared the van into reverse and backed up, spinning
the wheel and slicing our back bumper through the mob
in one clean motion. Zombies flew backward, smashing against each other only to pop back up, oblivious to
the injuries to their dead bodies. They weaved toward us
again like a limping collection of drunks to an overturned
beer truck.

We were facing the wrong way on the highway now…
not that it mattered. You could flip donuts on the I-5 in
L.A. now and not hit another car (not that we would be
so reckless…oh *no*, not us). Dave geared us forward and
slammed a few more zombies across our hood before he
swerved around and sped off toward the camp.

I heard dragging behind us, but after a while it faded. That happens a lot, actually. Zombie grabs your bumper, you speed off, find a dead broken zombie arm still clinging to the vehicle the next day. But it's not like zombies have insurance, so why stop for the accident, right?

"*That* was satisfying," I said with a sigh as we angled off the highway toward Tempe. "*And* you can add more to your steering wheel killing count."

"Not as satisfying as it will be when I find Jimmy," Dave said with a snarling sneer.

"There, there," I said with a light pat to his arm. "Next time we'll just let old No-Toes fend for himself. That's the only way he's ever going to learn."

"That or a massive ass-kicking."

"Well, if you do that, you'll get to practice your new karate moves, so it's a win-win, right?"

He chuckled. "Jujitsu, Sarah, not karate. Karate is like Trix. It's for kids."

"Wow, that was a particularly bad pun," I said with a shake of my head and a smile.

As the sun slowly set, he stared at nothing in particular until we left the highway. Since we'd come to Phoenix, this route had become second nature to us. Even if I closed my eyes, I knew the turns to get down the extra-wide streets to what was once the ASU campus and more specifically Sun Devil Stadium.

Of course, the zombies, the government, and the survivors had made a few alterations to the campus (and all without having a bond vote...who says the system doesn't work?).

With over seventy thousand students, professors, and other faculty at work and studying on the campus at the time of the outbreak, the zombies had ripped through the school like a black, drooling plague when the outbreak reached the city, about five days after its initial burst in Seattle. So while David and I were fleeing *our* city, *this* city had encountered its own version of hell just like so many others in the West.

So, the government had come with its planes and bombs and destroyed everything. Did it curb the zombies? Sort of. But I hated to think about how many survivors were taken out along with the living dead.

But those of us who were left were making our mark on the landscape now, too. As we turned down one of the more narrow streets that had once taken football fans to the parking lots near the stadium, we saw the wall.

Remember the big wall around the town in the second Mad Max movie? Well, it was kind of like that. Except without the faux-punk influences and the special kind of crazy that was Mel Gibson (who, by the way, I'd heard was turned into a zombie on like day four, though that might just be a rumor).

Constructed of debris, fencing, cars, anything that could be moved and stacked, really, had been placed around the caved-in walls of the camp to keep the zombies out and the people safe.

It worked most of the time, too. There had only been a few instances where zombies had either figured out how to scale the wall or someone infected had made it past inspection.

Dave shot me a look as the big gate (made of some kind of sheet metal siding as far as I could tell, with "New Phoenix" painted on it in bright yellow spray paint) slid open and allowed us into quarantine.

"Be nice," he said softly as he followed the gatekeeper's instruction to park to the left. "You pissed these guys off last time."

"One of those fuckers grabbed my boob to pose for a picture," I snapped as I glared at the small group of guys with their weapons ready outside my door.

David rolled his eyes. "He was just excited to meet the famous Zombiebusters. It's your fault with all your brand building and shit. You're Fucking Paris Hilton to these people."

I grimaced. "No, c'mon. Make me someone cool. Let me be... Anne Hathaway or Maggie Gyllenhaal."

"Okay, Indie Princess," he said with a shake of his head. "Whoever you are, be *good*."

I folded my arms. "I'll try, but the last guy is just lucky I didn't take off his hand."

Dave shook his head, but I'm pretty sure he smothered a smile even as we got out of the van. The gatekeeper, a guy name Smith, tilted his head in greeting as we moved around to the front of the vehicle. We'd left the lights on — that was standard procedure so that we could be checked. Or molested. Whichever was the case for the night.

"Hello David, Sarah," Smith said with another nod. "You know the drill."

We did, of course. Without much discussion we showed the checkers our arms, our legs, necks, anything that was a common target for zombies. They checked out clothes, too, and if there were rips or tears, you had to lift them up to verify you hadn't been bitten, but not yet turned. No one touched my chest, probably because I was using my mean glare. At least, that's my assumption. It might have also been because I kneed the last guy who did it in the balls.

Once they were satisfied with our status, Smith motioned the others away. I heard them whispering about Zombiebusters as they did so and I couldn't help but smile.

"You can park over there," Smith said, motioning to the line of cars in the white zone past the next gate, which was just a chain-link fence. "And lock your weapons in the car."

"Yeah, yeah," Dave said as he moved to the vehicle. "We know the drill."

He pulled the van through to parking but I stayed behind with Smith. He was a middle-aged guy with an air of ex-military about him. Maybe first Gulf War, though we never talked about it. The fact was, we were all soldiers now. There was no need to compare war wounds.

"Any news?" I asked.

Smith had the dusk-to-dawn shift at the gate and he always heard the first whiff of anything from the badlands as the survivors rolled into camp for the night.

He shrugged. "Just the usual. People yapping about the Midwest Wall, a few new pods here and there, that sort of thing."

He chuckled as he grabbed for a cigarette from his pocket. I noted he didn't light it, but just sucked on the filter. Not that I blamed him. Cigarettes were valuable in trade (which I have to admit, David had thought they would be when this all started and I'd given him shit about it). You couldn't just light up anymore.

Still, it was a shitty way to reduce the lung cancer rate.

"Oh, yeah," he said with a laugh. "Some loons are talking about special zombies."

I had been looking off past the second gate to see where

David had parked, but now I snapped my head around to look at Smith. "What do you mean 'special'?"

"Dunno," he said. My tone must have revealed something because he looked closer at me. "Just said they were different. Why?"

"Jimmy No-Toes said something similar about a pod in the Basilica," I said with a frown. "But all we found were regular droolers."

"Told you it was the kooks talking about it," Smith said with a shrug. "You can't exactly trust No-Toes."

"That's what David said, too," I said softly.

In the distance I saw Dave loading up a pack for our nightly supplies. As he locked up the van, he looked in my direction with an expression of confusion. Usually I only talked to Smith for a second or two.

"Well, he's likely right. Anyway, I see another car coming, gotta concentrate." Smith turned away. "'Night, Sarah."

"'Night."

I made my way through Gate 2 and joined David. He gave me the same questioning look I'd seen from a distance.

"What up?"

I shook my head. "Smith said that others were talking about 'different' zombies. Maybe bionics?"

David rolled his eyes. "C'mon. We didn't see anything *different* today. It's just freaked-out talk. Hell, I wouldn't put it past Jimmy and some of the others to even start that shit. It makes his goods more valuable if other people are too afraid to go out and find their own supplies."

I nodded. That made sense, actually. Jimmy had been a grifter in his past life, why not now when it was so much easier?

"Maybe you're right," I said as we walked down a sloping hill past what were once parking garages but now were flattened, twisted hulks of concrete and wire. "And there's always the fact that it's been a few months since the initial outbreak and people naturally have to scare themselves all over again."

"You'd think they'd have enough to be scared about," Dave said, trailing off as we entered the half-collapsed stadium itself.

We'd been staying here on and off for over a month now, but every time we came in it gave us pause. The makeshift camp held about five hundred survivors. I have to say, it was pretty well organized for being one of the biggest camps we'd seen. Some other camps had become a study in the worst of the Old West, with gunmen running the show, crime out of control, and people too afraid to speak out for fear they'd be left to the zombies as "punishment" for nameless offenses.

But here in New Phoenix they had formed a semblance of a government, a system to distribute supplies, and a trade market where one could haggle with anything from extra rations to grandma's silver (though rarely one's *own* grandma's silver). I guess that was all thanks to sensible people like Smith and some of the others who were in charge of this place.

We were lucky, but still, the stench of human sweat and waste was overpowering until the nose got used to it. And the people were tired, gaunt, and afraid, even if they tried to hide it. That was why we took our chances at least half the nights of the week and stayed outside the camp. It was just too hard to watch how low humanity had sunk in only a few months.

I blinked to keep sudden, always unexpected tears from falling and forced a smile. Someday this would get easier. It had to.

Didn't it?

"Come on, let's get dinner," Dave said softly as he took my hand. We didn't really talk about our feelings on the subject of the camps, but I knew him well enough to know it bugged him, too, no matter how jaded he pretended to be.

We weaved into the barracks area and grabbed some mismatched plates and cutlery before we got into line for chow. Swill. Whatever. Fresh food had vanished a long time ago, though you did sometimes scavenge your way into an orange grove or apple tree, which was always a nice surprise (and a valuable one here in camp).

Same thing with meat. Every blue moon you found a random cow or chicken you could actually catch to eat, though I guess that would end soon enough. Some History Channel thing about the end of the world had once said domesticated animals would die off pretty fast without people to make their lives easier (or harder). Stupid History Channel hadn't said much about how long we *humans* would live in a similar scenario.

But for sure the convenient little plastic trays with farmed meat wrapped in Saran Wrap were already a thing of the past. In the camps, we had canned goods, dried things, and sometimes not a ton of that. The cook on duty shoveled some beans onto my plate and a stale Pop-Tart (blueberry from the looks of a fake azure icing) and motioned us on our way. I sighed as we took a seat in the cafeteria tent and started to pick at the grub listlessly.

I was pretty fully into my funk when I looked across

the way and saw a little girl, probably no more than five, who was eating her Pop-Tart with enough gusto to make me smile. She smiled back and revealed teeth tinted blue from the icing, then dug into her beans.

The woman who was with the child just ran her fork through her food. She looked drawn and tired. She was probably a "camp-y" as we called them, people who had only lucked into survival of the initial outbreak, but hadn't actually learned to take care of themselves. Once camps were established, they stayed in them full-time and never ventured past the gates into the new outside world.

After such a long time of being penned in, they had a look about them. Actually, it was a lot like those cows the History Channel said were doomed.

The woman glanced down at the girl and her exhaustion seemed to fade as she smiled. They didn't look much alike — in fact I doubted they were related. It was entirely possible they had just found each other in the camp and formed a makeshift family right here. It happened a lot.

I was about to offer the child some of my Pop-Tart when there was a ruckus on the other side of me. I glanced over to find three big guys sitting down at the bench down the way. They were all talking at once as they slammed warm bottles of beer down beside their trays.

"Bigger than normals," one of them grunted. "With fangs."

"Ha!" another one said with a shake of his head. "I hear they can eat a man's head in two bites. If you think zombies are bad, they say these are worse. They might even be smart enough to storm the camp someday. Like a brainless army. Wipe us all out, that's what they'll do."

I glanced at the little girl and found she had huddled

closer to her mother, turning her face into the woman's chest, though the mother looked no less terrified by the overheard conversation.

"Hey!" I barked to the men. "You're scaring the kid."

The three glared at me for my interruption, but then one of them actually looked at the child and saw his foolishness was traumatizing. His expression softened and he shook his head.

"I'm sorry, honey," he said to the little girl. "We're just telling stories."

She didn't look convinced, nor did her mother as she gathered up their trays and moved off to a quieter corner.

"Smooth," Dave grunted as he shoveled the last of his beans down his throat.

The guys had the sense to look a little chagrined, but then they slid down the bench across the table to be closer to us.

"You're David and Sarah, right?" one of the younger men asked with a blush. "The Zombiebusters?"

David arched a brow my way as if to tell me, "I told you so," and then he nodded. "That's what the van says."

The men exchanged glances, apparently impressed. And I admit, my chest puffed out a little at the attention. I guess on some level I *was* more Paris Hilton than Maggie Gyllenhaal. So sue me!

"What have *you* heard about the special ones?" the same guy who had apologized to the little girl asked, but this time in a lower tone.

"C'mon." Dave rolled his eyes. "You guys are too old for fairy tales."

"They aren't fairy tales, man!" one of the men insisted. "This shit is real!"

Dave shook his head. "So I guess one of you has actually *seen* something out there beyond the normal, average zombies? Yourself, I mean."

That stopped them. They exchanged looks between their group and then the biggest one shrugged. "Uh, no."

"Let me guess. The people who told you this shit are the same ones who talk about the Midwest Wall and the government operatives who are coming to save us all just any old day now?"

I blinked at his harsh, sarcastic tone. These guys deserved his censure, don't get me wrong, but Dave had become pretty cynical since the outbreak. He'd gone from happy-go-lucky gamer to a hardened fighter.

He no longer believed anything anyone said about a place that was still safe or that anyone was eventually coming to fix this plague. And he didn't just dismiss pumped-up assholes like the ones sitting across from us now. Even if *I* mentioned the possibility of such stuff, he cut me off with a wave of his hand and a brusque change of subject.

But I have to tell you, even though I'd seen the same things he'd seen, been through the same shit he'd been through... I still held on to the slender reed of hope he'd managed to kill in himself.

I mean, it was *possible* They (whoever They were) *had* built a wall to separate the West from the East, a way to protect half the population from the outbreak, and if *They* had made the virus, or whatever it was that had started this nightmare, that *They* could fix it someday.

Right?

"Or maybe the ones who told you about 'different' zombies were the same ones who go on and on about cures and scientists?" Dave continued with a humorless laugh.

"I heard there really *are* some scientists working on the cure," the medium build of the three guys said, though he sounded less certain than he had when they all sat down. "Maybe even in protected labs right here in the West."

Dave let his fork hit his plate with a clatter. "Pipe dreams, boys. You should know better by now. What we can trust are the things we can see. Weapons, the camps, a vehicle that still has half a tank of fuel. That shit is real. Everything else . . ." He waved his hand in the air. "Illusion. Like Santa and the Tooth Fairy."

The men shifted uncomfortably and Dave returned his attention to my plate.

"Done?" he asked.

I ate the last few bites and nodded. "Yeah."

"I'm beat. Let's find a tent and call it good." He grabbed my plate and my hand, gave the now silent and sullen men a quick nod, and we took off toward the exit.

As he set our dishes into an overflowing tray, I gave him a side look. "You know, there *may* still be some good in the world. I wish you wouldn't give up on that idea entirely."

He didn't answer as we entered the tent city area of the camp. A few hundred tents, scavenged and traded by survivors, were set up in long rows that repeated and repeated out in front of us. There were everything from small child-sized ones with Dora the Explorer's tattered, stained face on the outside, to orange ones a family probably once took out into the mountains for a weekend, to military-grade outfits that slept ten or twelve people.

Dave paused as he scanned a sign-up sheet by the sleeping area for a tent that had two cots available. Once he had found one and had marked it as taken, he began steering me in that direction.

I figured he wasn't going to respond to what I'd said, but as we ducked into the tent he'd signed us up for (a four-man sleeper), he turned toward me.

"Look, it's not that I have no hope. I believe there's plenty of 'good' right here. And we're doing okay, right? The infected are a lot less active toward us now, and we've got a pretty fucking good system for killing them. We're together and that's what matters to me."

He hesitated and here came the *but*.

"*But* I have no illusions that all that bullshit about a future without these monsters is going to happen. They wiped out the entire West in about two weeks, Sarah. There's no way they could be stopped. Not by a wall or a scientist toiling in some borderline cartoon lab. I just can't waste too much energy praying and looking for it."

I stared at him, uncertain how to respond when he laid out a future for us that held nothing but faint reassurance that we'd survive, but never get back to any kind of normal life.

Luckily, I didn't have to answer, because at that moment another couple entered the tent to claim the other two cots in the room. I forced a smile because we knew the two of them a little and liked them even more.

Josh and Drea, who had found each other a few weeks after the outbreak (though they were so perfect together that you'd never know they hadn't been together for ten years). They were about our age and shared a similar and rather snarky sense of humor with us. We had exchanged some zombie-killing stories that had left us sobbing with laughter.

"Hi guys," Josh said with a broad smile you hardly ever saw on a survivor. But his good humor was somehow still intact even after the hell of infection and death. "We saw your names on the sheet and figured we'd share a tent tonight."

Dave forced a quick smile, but I thought I saw a little relief in his eyes. Like he didn't really want to talk to me about the unknown future anymore.

"So you guys hear anything new?" Dave asked as he took off the backpack he'd grabbed from our van and started laying out our blankets and inflatable pillows for the night.

Drea shrugged as she smoothed pieces of her pixie-cut blond hair out of her pretty face. "Naw. Just the usual. Death, maiming, destruction, killing the walking dead. You know. Same old, same old."

"Well, TGIF, right?" I laughed.

"Is it Friday?" Josh asked.

I shrugged. "I don't know. I lost track months ago."

We all grinned, even Dave, and then Drea asked, "Did you see you have a message on the board?"

I looked at Dave. Normally we checked the big tack board in the center of the camp as soon as we got in, but tonight we'd both been distracted.

"A call for an exterminator?" Dave asked as he flopped down on his cot with an exhausted sigh.

Drea shrugged. "I don't know. It didn't say specifically."

I tilted my head in surpise. Normally messages for us were pretty fucking clear. Like, "get the fuck over here, there are zombies" kind of clear.

"Do you want to go look?" I asked Dave.

He shook his head. "Not now. We'll do it tomorrow."

We talked for a little while. These two had the *best* stories... and not just zombie ones. I mean ones that made us all forget zombies even for a little bit. I don't know what Josh did before the outbreak, but Drea had owned a restaurant in L.A. that had attracted all kinds of celebrities. She had stories about famous people... well, they were pretty entertaining.

But eventually exhaustion took over and we blew out the Coleman lantern.

With the end of electricity, people had quickly returned to the schedules of the farm days, rising at dawn, working during the light, and returning "home" at dusk to turn in. Within minutes of the light going out, the other three exhaled deep, heavy breaths.

But I couldn't sleep. I kept thinking about bionic zombies and the Midwest Wall and a thousand other thoughts Dave wanted me to forget so I could live in the now. But the *now* sucked big time. I couldn't just forget that and go to sleep like he could.

With a sigh, I pushed out of the sleeping bag and put on my boots. I grabbed a flashlight and finally slipped out of the tent into the night air.

CHAPTER 4

Be proactive...and ready to run
if proactive backfires.

Phoenix may be warm during the day in November, but it's brisk at night and I immediately regretted not grabbing my jacket as I used a sputtering, blinking flashlight to guide me out of the sleeping area. Pretty soon the battery would be dead and we'd have to use another precious one in our dwindling supply. With a frown, I turned off the light and headed toward the center of camp by the light of the full moon overhead instead.

It was weird how much little things changed after an apocalypse. Big things, yeah, you expected those, but the tiny shit still took me off guard. For instance, six months ago if you'd taken a stroll around the campus here at night you would have heard cars on the streets, the yells of frat boys screaming drunken boasts and making general asses of themselves, even planes flying in and out of the airport, which wasn't too far away. Basically lots of background noise that indicated a certain kind of life.

But now other sounds were clearer. Outside the walls

of the camp, coyotes moaned and howled as they retook their territory and crickets chirped in the stillness. Humans still had a place though. In the distance I heard the light strum of guitars and the faint sounds of singing that made my heart stutter a little.

The van only had an eight track that was long dead, so we hardly ever got to hear music. I came to a stop as I left the tent area and just listened to the tones of "Come as You Are" by Nirvana, with a faint female voice singing the lyrics softly.

I shook my head with nostalgia as I strode forward again toward the big board in the middle of the camp. I found it by the campfire lights and the moon, but reading the little notes and requests was too hard without additional light, so I reluctantly turned my flashlight back on.

In the stark light of the bare bulb, the messages on the board seemed even sadder, just as they had in the church. There were plenty of faded ones looking for people who were missing. Some had been there for over a month (at least as long as we'd been coming here) and were obviously pleas for people who would never be found or at least not found *alive*. Undead maybe, but that wasn't a good end for anyone involved.

Finally, through the mass of notes asking for specific food items and one particularly disturbing request for a sex doll and some lube (um, ew, people. Just...*ew*), I found a note addressed to Zombiebusters Exterminators, Inc (the *whole* name, no less). I pulled it from the board and examined it closely.

It was written on heavy paper, something far more expensive than the back of newspapers or cheap notebook sheets most people used. The author had neat, even handwriting and the pen he or she used was red.

Blood red words on a stark white sheet. Gee, obvious horror music playing in the background, anyone?

Still, a job was a job and this one was intriguing:

"I am in need of your assistance for a unique task. If you can accommodate me, please meet with me. Sincerely, A Friend."

An address followed, one I didn't instantly recognize even after all our exploration of the dead city and its surrounding areas. Looked like the old GPS was going to get some use.

Oh yeah, GPS satellites? Turns out they don't go down, even when most of the people on earth (or at least *this* part of earth) get eaten by a shambling horde of monsters. Just an FYI.

I stuffed the note into my pocket and headed back toward our tent, but my mind was still clouded with thoughts. Most of the time our "services" got repeat offenders. People we knew asked us to clear out a shed or wipe out an apartment building filled with the living dead.

But this... this was a whole new person (or people) with a "unique" task, whatever that meant. It could be dangerous. And not just "zombie dangerous," but like... "don't go down there!" dangerous.

Sadly, as I stepped back into our tent and climbed into my sleeping bag, the concept of a whole new kind of dangerous gave me a thrill I hadn't felt in a long time.

"So you just went out into the night all by yourself?" Dave snapped as he practically ripped the passenger door of the van off before he got inside.

"Yes," I grunted as I slammed the driver's side door of the van and started the engine a bit more loudly than was probably necessary. "As I have mentioned to you about thirty times since we woke up this morning, *that* is correct."

"It was a stupid thing to do, Sarah."

With a shake of his head, he pulled out a GPS unit from the glove compartment (kept right beside a nice collection of 9mm handguns and ammo—yup, we were pretty much right out of Bonnie and Clyde now...minus the bank robberies and the Faye Dunaway hair). He jammed the plug into our ancient cigarette lighter and waited for the satellite to link up.

"I don't get what you're freaking out about," I said with a heavy, put-upon sigh. "I got up, *in camp.*"

"How *silly* of me," Dave said, his voice laced with the same blunt sarcasm he'd used last night with the idiots who'd been talking about bionics. "There's just *nothing* dangerous lurking around in camp."

I shook my head. "Okay, I know it isn't perfectly safe. But shit, it's not like I put on some flip-flops and headed out into the desert to do some zombie skeet shooting. Chill."

He folded his arms and flopped back against the seat without further comment. Ah, pouting. Still hot in the living dead universe. Or not.

I ignored the silent treatment as I snatched the GPS from the dash and entered the address from the note we'd been left in camp. After a couple more seconds of load time it started a "route to" sequence. I put the van in gear and eased it into the line of vehicles heading out of the camp and into the new day. We were a ragtag little group, too, consisting of everything from fancy, high-end sports cars to beaters.

Both of these extremes were totally useless, by the way. A sporty car looked cool and all, but it did nothing unless you intended to keep it on the highway and scream along like a bat out of hell.

The beaters were useless, too — always breaking down, needing special parts and attention. And they were *weird*, honestly. After all, one of the coolest things in an apocalypse was that you could have any ride you want — and trust me, David and I had tested that theory multiple times (oh, the Jag, don't get me started on the Jag — *heaven*!) before settling on our awesome van. So why anyone would *choose* to ride in a Gremlin with a window taped shut or a lopsided pickup whose floorboards were rotted through was beyond me.

Eventually we got out of the camp and after about twenty minutes of driving down the highway, Dave seemed to perk up. He sat up and clicked the GPS off its stand. Flipping buttons, he looked at the turn-by-turn route info while I drove.

"Take next exit, then turn left" the bland, computerized female voice ordered.

I stifled a laugh. The whole GPS unit thing had never been a perfect system, even before the world went to hell. I mean, we'd been led astray by them a few times on vacations and ended up God knew where (once, I swear it took us to a cult compound when we wanted to go to Olive Garden).

But in a zombie reality, it was even worse. The unit now gave directions to places which no longer existed on roads that had been riddled with bombs or still had asphalt streaked with blood or ooze. Sometimes there wasn't a "right turn" to be made thanks to a sinkhole or zombie hive.

Or in this case, the exit in question had experienced some "unreported technical difficulties."

Namely that a truck with ridiculously oversized rims was turned broadside at the top of the ramp to block it off. By the rusted, bloody, sludgy look of the vehicle, this had been done months ago, maybe even at the beginning of the outbreak, perhaps in some lame attempt to keep the zombie horde from swarming into the area.

"Apparently they thought the infected would come in buses?" Dave asked with his own chuckle as we stared at the makeshift barricade.

"Right, like the oldsters during winter," I said with a nod as I brought the van to a stop at the top of the exit. "Zombie Airways flew them down on a $99-each-way special and brought them all down to the resorts and condos for a break. Zombie life is *hard* up North."

When Dave looked at me with that little twinkle in his eye at my comment, I knew he wasn't pissed at me anymore for going off by myself last night.

"I'll see if I can move her," he said with a sigh.

I turned off our engine and got out with a rifle in hand. I kept an eye out for stragglers while Dave tried the door on the truck. When he pulled the handle, the entire door came off in his hand. He staggered under the unexpected weight and went down on one knee as he tossed the broken piece of metal aside. It shrieked as it skidded across the asphalt and onto the shoulder.

"What the fuck?" he snapped to no one in particular as he got back up and rubbed his wrist absently.

"You okay?" I asked, doing another perimeter check through the scope on the .357.

He grunted. "I guess, but what in the world would make the door come off like that?"

He leaned down and looked at the door hinges and then stood back up. "Only thing I see is sludge. Since when does sludge cut through metal enough to rot a door off?"

Cautiously, I moved to the big truck and looked at the evidence myself. Sure enough, the metal hinges that had held the door in place seemed to have been sheared off, eroded by some kind of chemical.

"It can't just be the sludge," I said with a shake of my head, because that was the only thing I saw on the broken metal, too. "I mean, maybe the door was already damaged or they did this as a weird booby trap or something."

Dave looked at the vehicle absently. "Yeah, I guess."

"Be careful when you try to move it, though," I added with a look at the truck from front to back. "If somebody did something to jimmy the door, maybe they did something else, too."

Of course there were no keys. Would it really be that easy? So instead of starting the truck and pulling it off the ramp, Dave put it in neutral and with a bunch of effort we managed to shove the hunk of rusting metal into motion, despite two deflated tires we hadn't noticed on first inspection.

With a lot of grunting and swearing, we guided it toward the side edge of the ramp. The big, heavy body hit the guard rail with a scrape of metal on metal and then an ominous creak and crash as the badly maintained rail gave under the strain. The truck teetered on the edge of the embankment for a long moment, and then it rolled clear down the dusty hill onto a service road below where it landed, crushed nose down, in the middle of the street.

We stared down at it for a long moment and then we exchanged a rather evil little grin. Yeah, even after all these months it was still pretty fun to destroy property without fear of the consequences. I think in another life David and I had been anarchists.

Sort of like zombies, I guess...

But for now I stared at the broken, busted truck with a sense of accomplishment and satisfaction. Especially when I noticed that the mud flaps had those cheesy silhouettes of naked girls.

Nice.

"Onward," I proclaimed as we hopped back in the van and followed the GPS system's insistent directions that we take the next exit, then turn left.

We drove for another fifteen minutes through rapidly decreasing city into an ominously quiet area I'd never visited before. It was dead desert, except for a few spotty trailers here and there and some dilapidated buildings that appeared to have been damaged even before the apocalypse.

Now *why* did I keep hearing the theme from *Deliverance* in my head?

"Arrive at your destination in a quarter-mile, on the right," the GPS declared and then went quiet, its job done unless we did something stupid and went off course, at which point the voice would come back on and tell us to "please turn back" or "recalculating" over and over until I wanted to scream. I'd broken three GPSes over this issue already, you know. David was starting to get annoyed by it.

I slowed the vehicle to a crawl as we rolled up on our "destination," though you could hardly call it that. It had once been a warehouse of some kind, but not a nice one. You know those flimsy steel siding "make-it-yourself" type buildings you used to see advertised in local commercials all the time? Well, this was one of those and it looked like it had been through hell.

Blood slashed down the sides of the once-white metal, combining with rust to make an eerie orange-red pattern on a rotting metal canvas. The roof was half caved in and the eastern wall had collapsed against itself and sagged precariously. A stiff wind and the whole structure was bound to fall down around the head of anyone who dared take shelter inside.

Any idiot who looked at the place would think the same. So *why* had we been called here?

"I don't like this," Dave muttered at my side as he took the safety off his rifle.

I shook my head slowly. "Me neither, but we're here now. Should we check it out?"

He gave me a half-glance but I couldn't read his guarded expression. "I don't know, Sarah..."

I pursed my lips and bit my tongue so I wouldn't say something sarcastic. I got the need to be cautious, I really did, but the more I stared at the building, the more I wanted to know who had called us here and what was waiting inside.

"Please?" I begged as I turned to face Dave. I batted my eyelashes and tilted my head.

He laughed despite the worry in his eyes. "Um, okay. But let's gear up solid and stay sharp. I just..." he looked at the building with a faraway look, "have a bad feeling about this."

I groaned at the familiar line. "Okay, you can quote *Star Wars* but only because you agreed to come with me."

Again he laughed as we got out of the van and eased our way to the back where we loaded up on weapons, from guns to stabbing and clubbing items. I shut the van doors as quietly as possible and then we crept toward the warehouse in a slow, steady military formation we'd read about in a library book about Navy SEALs.

Of course there was a difference between reading about SEALs and being them. One we quickly recognized when I stepped on some kind of trip wire hidden in the dust and suddenly about ten guns, all of them military grade (including one *sweet* cannon I totally wished I could steal without getting shot) and meant to fire multiple shots in a matter of seconds, appeared from hidden cubbies all around the warehouse. And they were all pointed at us.

David froze, reaching back to pull me closer to his back as if he could protect me from hundreds of speeding bullets. Kind of sweet, though not particularly well thought out.

"What the fuck?" he growled.

Before I could respond to what was clearly a rhetorical question, the bent warehouse door ahead of us opened and a man in a lab coat and a pair of wire-rimmed glasses appeared in the entryway. He blinked a few times, like he wasn't accustomed to the sun, and then stepped into the desert with his own weapon raised to match the others all around us.

His was impressive, too. A fully automatic AK-47, definitely not legal before the zombie outbreak. He held it like he knew how to use it, despite his geeked-out attire.

As he moved a few cautious steps closer, I noticed he

was pretty young. Probably just a handful of years older than us. *Maybe* mid-thirties?

Another thing that hit me right away was that he was clean. Not spit-shine clean like most of us, but *really* clean. I swear I could smell the soapy scent of his skin and the fresh detergent of his clothing even from here and it was like heaven.

He was cute, too. I'll admit it. He kind of had a Luke Wilson in *The Royal Tenenbaums* (rather than Luke Wilson hyping cell phones) vibe about him that made me blink a couple of times despite the fact that he had a gun in my face and apparently had some kind of control over a whole bunch more.

"I'm sorry to do this," he called out. "But I *do* have the power to pull all these triggers at once so I hope you won't be rash. Simply do as I say and allow me the time to explain myself and I won't have to use this."

He lifted some kind of remote from his pocket that apparently operated the weapons around us, then slipped it back into his shirt pocket and returned his finger to the trigger of the gun he held.

"What the hell is wrong with you?" Dave snapped, still holding me against his back in a big old hero pose. "*You* called *us* here!"

I stared at the guy over Dave's shoulder, still intrigued by the dichotomy of the cute face, the nerdy jacket, and the big-ass gun.

"Didn't you?" I asked.

The guy nodded. "Oh yes, I did indeed ensure that a message was posted for you at the New Phoenix survivor camp, though I didn't post it myself."

"Then why the fuck are you pointing a gun—"

"A shitload of guns," I interrupted.

Dave shot me a look over his shoulder. "Pardon me, a *shitload* of guns at us?"

"I am very happy to explain," the man said. "But first I have to insist that you disarm yourselves fully and come into the warehouse."

"Disarm ourselves," Dave said softly, so only I could hear. "Is he nuts?"

I looked at our captor. He didn't have the wild look about him that some people did after everything we'd all been through. That didn't mean he wasn't nuts, of course, just that he was able not to show it as clearly as say... Jimmy No-Toes.

"What choice do we have?" I asked.

Dave looked at the guy for a long moment and I could see the wheels turning in his mind, looking for a way out of this just like he'd found a way out of dozens of other situations over the past few months.

"Those guns might not even be attached to that remote," he finally said.

I shrugged, though his suggestion didn't make me feel all that much better. "I guess it's possible. And even if they are, he called us here so he must need us. Maybe he won't really press the button. But do you want to test it?"

Apparently he did because Dave lifted his gun to his shoulder and pointed it at the lab coat guy. "I don't think so, asswipe. Instead, I think you're going to let us back away and get into our van."

"Please David," Lab Coat said. "I really don't think that would be wise. Just come inside and I swear to you that I'll explain everything to you and Sarah."

But Dave wasn't going to agree just because the guy

knew our names. Like I said before, it wasn't that shocking thanks to our minor celebrity status in the local area. People called us by our first names all the time.

Most of them just weren't pointing a gun . . . I'm sorry, a *shitload* of guns . . . at us. Dave shook his head and started inching backward toward the van. With a grimace, Lab Coat Guy reached into his pocket and pressed a button. In unison the guns around us cocked or their safety measurements slid off.

I flinched. Shit, that thing really *did* control the weapons mounted at every conceivable angle.

"David . . ." I whispered.

But to my surprise, he wasn't paying attention to the fact that we were about to get shot. Instead, he had turned his head and was looking back over his shoulder. Past the van, into the distance. Shaking, I turned my attention to whatever had caught his eye and let out a little shriek.

A swarm of zombies crested a small hill in the road we had come up to find this place. There were probably at least a hundred, some jogging, others just shambling their way toward us without any real drive or purpose. Already I could hear their groaning moans and hisses of hunger.

"You see, the situation is deteriorating with every moment you wait," Lab Coat Guy said as we returned our stares to him. He was looking past us at the coming zombie horde, too, and a sheen of sweat had broken out on his upper lip. "If I don't allow you to leave, you'll be eaten. Or I'll have to shoot you. Either scenario doesn't end well for you. So please, come inside and let me take care of that lot."

Dave looked at me and back at the horde. They were within a tenth of a mile now. I could almost smell the death on their breath.

"Shit," he muttered. "Drop everything and run, Sarah. Go inside!"

Within seconds, we shed our weapons in a pile at our feet and ran toward the warehouse. The faster zombies had reached us by that time and were at our heels. I felt their fingers brush my back as I rushed past the stranger who now held our lives in his hands. And then there was only the sound of automatic gunfire.

I spun around as we got behind him to find that Lab Coat Guy had depressed the button in his pocket. All the guns on the turrets fired at once, hitting the zombies in one continuous shot. The living dead lurched and danced with the impact of the bullets on their chests and more importantly, heads, then fell into briefly moaning piles of sludge and goo.

Lab Coat Guy turned toward us, his face impassive and almost bored. For a guy who had called on a pair of exterminators, he had extermination down pretty pat already.

"Well, now that *that* messy business is taken care of," he said with a sheepish smile. "Do you have any other weapons I need to know about? Perhaps hidden in a shoe or inside your clothing?"

I frowned before I bent and pulled a knife from one boot and an old-fashioned Derringer Dave and I had thought was hilarious from the other. Dave removed the gun belt he wore under his shirt and we dropped them all at our feet.

"Very good," Lab Coat said with a smile. "Why don't you come with me?"

David glared and I couldn't help doing the same. After all, the guy was still pointing his AK-47 at us.

"Come *with* you?" Dave snapped as he looked around

us in the dark and dusty building that was decidedly empty. "Where to exactly?"

With a smile, Lab Coat Guy backed slowly to the far wall of the warehouse. He picked up a big metal box with a red button and a green button on its face. With his thumb, he pressed the green button and suddenly the floor right in front of David and I opened and a platform lifted up from beneath it.

"What the hell?" Dave snapped.

Lab Coat Guy moved forward, weapon still raised and ready. "I know you have questions. Just come with me. I promise all this will soon make sense."

Dave tensed and I could see he was about to go ape shit on this guy. I turned toward him and caught his arm, squeezing gently as I looked up into his eyes.

"We've gone this far," I whispered. "And the fact that he's *asking* us to do this seems like a formality. He *is* holding the gun."

Dave looked down at me, then back at our new "friend." "The second I get a chance, I'm going to punch you square in the face, motherfucker."

Lab Coat Guy smiled indulgently. "Duly noted. Now please step onto the platform."

We all did and with a press of his foot on another button, Lab Coat lowered us down into a dark chasm. The doors above us closed and we rode down, down, down for what seemed like forever. The darkness was complete for half the ride and then it started to change. Muted green bulbs appeared on the walls, then red ones, then white.

White light. From electricity. Something we hadn't seen for months (I guess I figured Lab Coat's different remotes were operated by batteries). We both blinked, shocked by the glow of the bulbs as the lift came to a stop inside a protected steel cage. Through the metal grating I saw something that nearly stopped my heart. Something that made me shake as I backed up against David's chest and felt my knees give out just a little.

We were in a lab. A real fucking lab with glass rooms and pristine white halls and *lights*, so many lights!

Lab Coat Guy gave us a brief smile before he released a latch at the cage door and swung it open to allow us all entry into a sterile hallway.

Dave and I stood on the lift, just staring for a long moment before Lab Coat Guy said, "Well? Are you coming or are you just going to stand there staring?"

With a shake of his head like he was waking from a dream, Dave grasped my hand and we stepped into the hallway together to follow Lab Coat Guy down the hallway toward an uncertain future.

"There's only one explanation for this," I whispered as we turned at a T-Intersection in the hallway and our new "friend" slid a card through a key lock. At the end of the passage, a white door opened silently. "We've been attacked and *this* is how zombies see the world."

Dave looked down at me with a shiver at the possibility that what I said might actually be true.

"Right now we're probably eating a Girl Scout troop," I finished with a nervous grimace.

"Don't be silly," Lab Coat Guy said as he looked over his shoulder at us. "There haven't been any Girl Scouts for months. And you aren't zombies. This is entirely real, I assure you. And now"—he slowly lowered his gun at his side—"let me introduce myself. My name is Kevin Barnes. *Dr.* Kevin Barnes. And this is my lab."

We both stared, shocked into silence (rare for us, I assure you). Finally it was Dave who looked down at me, his face pale and his eyes wide.

"I-I guess I was wrong," he stammered. "It turns out there *are* mad scientists after all."

CHAPTER 5

Don't fear change. Just fear everything
and everyone else.

Dr. Barnes chuckled as he gave Dave a look that was normally reserved for silly children.

"Oh no, David. Not a mad scientist, I'm merely a scientist."

"I'm sure that's just what Dr. Frankenstein said right before he made a zombie of his own," I whispered.

I was sort of shocked I could find enough of my voice for that. I was still half-convinced this was all a fucked-up dream brought on by too many beans and Pop-Tarts. Was this what scurvy did to a person? I'd have to look it up in one of our medical books as soon as I woke up from this whacked-out dream.

"Please, come in," Dr. Barnes insisted as he passed through the door his key card had unlocked. "I'll try to explain everything to you."

We followed him. I guess we were too numb and curious to do anything else. Inside we found a tidy office, sort of like what you used to find at a clinic before you went into an exam room. There was a big desk near the back wall with a computer on it. A computer that was on and working! Instantly all my little geek-centricities kicked in and I longed to check e-mail and see what was up with I Can Has Cheezburger.

Of course, those things didn't exist anymore, computer or not.

In the back of the room and along the left wall were banks of windows, but built-in blinds were lowered between the panes of glass to keep us from seeing what was on the other side.

The room was cool, probably half from being underground and half from the air conditioning pumping through vents hidden somewhere in the room. Air conditioning! We hadn't felt that in months (again, old vans have their advantages and disadvantages).

Soft light glowed from a desk lamp beside the desk and some kind of instrumental music drifted out of the computer speakers.

It was all like a weird oasis from what was just above us.

Dr. Barnes took a place at his desk and motioned us to sit across from him. As we sank into the seats and stared, both of us too stunned to do much else, he smiled.

"You must have a few questions."

Dave snorted as a response, but Barnes ignored his interruption.

"Let me begin at the beginning. You see, this warehouse was once owned by a government facility for which I worked."

Dave shifted in his chair as we shot each other a look. Governmental lab. Sort of like the one at the University of Washington where all this shit started.

"Making zombies, were we, Doc?" I asked softly.

Barnes's face paled at least three shades and I thought he might pass out right then and there. He was filled with righteous indignation when he sputtered, "Of course not!"

"Then what *were* you doing way out in the desert in a warehouse obviously designed to look like a nothing hole?" Dave asked, his brow arching.

"We — well, it was classified," the other man stammered as his eyes darted away from us. "And it really doesn't matter now, does it?"

"Doesn't it?" I asked as I folded my arms. "Damn, I don't want to find out there's something worse out there waiting to be unleashed on us."

Barnes hesitated. "Well, if there is, it wasn't something I was involved in before the infection. And whatever I did before, there's no longer a government to work for, at least not out here. I'm no different than you two now."

Dave opened his mouth to argue, but I jumped in instead. "So how did you survive the outbreak?"

The doctor's frown deepened. "When the infection began, a few of my assistants and I were downstairs in this lab. An emergency lockdown procedure was triggered at the first whiff of those *things* hitting the city and we were trapped with only satellite television to tell us the story of what was going on just twenty feet above us."

I flinched. As bad as it had been to be a part of the outbreak, I could hardly imagine being physically trapped somewhere, only able to watch on monitors while all the horror unfolded just above you. It must have been like a bad movie . . . except you couldn't change the channel.

"But after a couple of days, the television stations from

around the world slowly broke out and then died. Even the military links failed, which is when we all recognized just how bad it had gotten." He sighed.

I tilted my head to look at him. If this was an act, he was very fucking good at it. Like "I'd like to thank the Academy" good.

"So how'd you get out, *Doc*?" Dave asked, seemingly less impressed than I was. His arms were folded tightly in front of him and his eyes were narrowed.

"After about a week, the power went out up above, which unlocked the elevator. After much debate, we went into the world to see what was happening. And found..." Barnes shuddered. "Well, what now exists...out there."

"So how many of you are there?" Dave asked. "We haven't seen anyone else since our arrival."

"I'm afraid the only one left is...me." Barnes dipped his chin to stare at his desk. He pulled off his glasses and once again the pain in his eyes seemed real, at least to me. "The rest were tragically killed either by injury or infection before we were able to figure out the warehouse's hidden defense system that you two encountered today."

I bit my lip. I sort of felt sorry for the guy, but I still had questions. *Lots* of questions.

"So if you have a defense system and this lab apparently has some kind of generated power —" I began.

"Natural," the doctor interrupted proudly. "We fully run on solar, which as you know is still in high supply here in Arizona. It's the highest tech there is for natural power production."

I nodded, somewhat impressed but unwilling to show it. "Whatever, my point is that with all you have in your little fortress...why do you need us? Why *did* you call us here and set up this whole ambush? You obviously don't need a couple of two-bit exterminators."

"Hey," Dave said with a glare in my direction. "I'm at least three-bit."

"Sorry." I smiled at him. "What do you want with one two-bit and one three-bit exterminator?"

The doctor seemed less than amused by our witty, sparkling banter. "Because you see, I know how to kill these...*things*."

"Zombies."

He flinched. "A rather pedestrian term, but if you insist. I know how to kill these zombies with the protection system at the lab, but what I *need* is someone to catch them. Alive. And bring them back here to me."

Dave and I stared blankly at the man, stunned into silence. Then to my surprise, David started to laugh. Like full-on laugh and it wasn't hysterical.

"Okay, that's funny," he said with a shake of his head. "What a set-up, too, for Candid Camera. Fake a zombie apocalypse, nearly kill us, *actually* kill about a million... or ten million or a hundred million...other people and all to get us here for the big punch line."

"David, I assure you—" the other man began.

But Dave wasn't done yet. He looked at me with a slightly maniacal grin. "Did you hear him, babe? *Catch a zombie*. Where's Allen Funt? I just can't wait to break both his arms."

"Honey, Allen Funt is dead."

He scowled. "During the zombie outbreak?" he asked.

"No, back in the '90s, I think," I offered with a shrug.

Despite the teasing, I reached out and touched Dave's arm to squeeze it gently. He had already threatened to pop this guy in the mouth, now I could see, behind his false joviality, that he was pretty fucking close to rearranging pretty boy doctor's face and making him look more like Owen Wilson than Luke.

"You don't believe me and I can't say I blame you," Barnes said, remarkably calm in the face of David's subtle, yet pulsating, rage and our mutual mocking. "So let me *show* you that I'm perfectly serious."

Reaching behind him, Barnes depressed a button and the shade on the window at the back of the room lifted to reveal a small room. Inside was a line of cages containing a small collection of guinea pigs, some alone in their holding cells, others in small pods. Each one had a tag in their ear and what looked like a small painted or dyed marking on their fur. Three dots and a line at the end.

I stared. "Really? *Actual* guinea pigs? Is this the cliché lab or what?"

Barnes ignored me. "We were using them for other types of research, but since the plague, I've switched my focus. Now..."

He pressed a few buttons on a computer nearby and suddenly robotic arms swung out from a folded position in the corner of the room. With a few delicate maneuvers, they reached into one of the cages and caught a fat, red guinea pig who was roaming around by himself.

The animal didn't seem bothered by the sudden intrusion. It continued to chew on a bit of feed, staring with an empty expression at nothing in particular. As one arm held it, the other lifted a syringe and injected the little animal right at its neck, then set it back into the cage gently.

"This is the infected blood from a..." Barnes sighed, heavy and put-upon, "*zombie*."

We all watched as the animal began to convulse. It flopped helplessly for a few agonizing moments, but just as suddenly it went still and limp against the cage floor. Within seconds, it got back up.

I couldn't help but flinch because we had seen this so many times before, although always in people, which was worse... so much worse. Although I have to say, a zombiefied guinea pig was pretty hideous, too.

The creature's beady eyes were now red as it lunged toward the cage edge and snarled and bit at the guinea pigs in the adjoining cage. The other little animals cowered back, huddling in a group that put me in mind of the camp just a short drive away.

Black sludge poured from the poor infected creature's mouth and it banged its head against the bars of its cage in an attempt to get into the other cage and satisfy its craving for... um, guinea pig soufflé, I guess.

"So you *can* make an animal into a zombie," I whispered.

The ramifications of that were horrifying. Small animals, small spaces to hide in — the risk of infection had just gone up. The chances of survival... not so much.

"Yes," Barnes said with a solemn shake of his head. "But it doesn't appear to happen in any natural environment I've studied. The outbreak began in humans and the infected only seem to attack their own kind. So far that means the animals have been safe."

"Until they start eating the rotting flesh from zombies," Dave muttered.

My heart sank at the idea, but Barnes looked at me with a small smile that was somehow comforting. "Actually, there is something in the smell of the infected that puts animals off. I've observed them devouring the flesh from dead who were uninfected by the outbreak, but not the corpses of the ... *zombies*. At least so far."

I nodded slowly. That was something at least. So far.

"Now, let me show you what I've developed," the doctor muttered, almost to himself.

He flipped another switch and the robotic arms returned to the cage. The infected animal lunged for them this time, biting them mercilessly until they caught his little writhing body and lifted him to inject him a second time. Through the glass we couldn't hear the sound, but it opened its mouth in what seemed like a howl of pain and frustration (if a guinea pig, especially one who is now a zombie, can feel such an emotion) as he was set back into his isolated cage.

At first nothing happened. The littlest zombie merely paced around and around its enclosure, heaving in breaths and occasionally throwing itself toward the cage bars as if it was testing their strength.

But, after about two minutes, its breathing rate slowed almost back to normal. The little creature stopped attacking the bars and instead returned to its dish of pellets and picked up a few to munch on. When the robotic hands returned to the cage and picked it up, it hardly registered a reaction. Slowly, they pulled the guinea pig to the other cage with the herd of other animals and deposited it within their ranks.

We were holding our collective breath as the once-infected animal not only didn't attack the others, but merged into their group without so much as a growl in their direction. Apparently forgetful of their friend's recent terrifying attempt to turn them into guinea pig steaks (a diet craze that will soon sweep the nation, I'm sure), they welcomed him back to the fold (by ignoring him, but that's as good as it gets with guinea pigs, I think).

Dave was the first one to break the silence. "How long does he stay like that?"

The doctor looked at us, eyes wide and filled with unmistakable triumph. "So far, permanently."

I blinked. "What?"

"There are animals in that cage that were treated a week ago and have shown no signs of cannibalistic tendencies."

"Were all of them infected at some point—could that be why they're calm?" I asked, still staring at the apparently happy little group.

"I understand what you're asking," Barnes said with a shake of his head. "The infected don't seem to attack each other. But no, there are five control animals in the pen that have never been infected. It—it's a cure. Or at least it might be."

Dave stared at him. "What do you mean *might* be?"

"I haven't yet had a chance to test it on human subjects. Ones who are currently infected. *That* is why I require live specimens." Barnes stared off at the cage again. "I've done some work on the heads of the deceased zombies in order to study brain chemistry and other elements, but—"

My eyes went wide as I thought of all the times we'd been told to bring back "evidence" of our kills by the people who had hired us. And that fact didn't slip past Dave either.

"Wait, what?" Dave asked, his eyes narrowing until I was pretty sure he couldn't see out of them at all. "You did work on *heads*? Is that why so many of our clients have been demanding we bring the heads of the zombies back? To give to *you*? Exactly how many people know about your little lab?"

Barnes stood up and I watched as his hand slid over to touch the AK-47 that now rested on his desk top. I got to my own feet, hoping to defuse the situation if it escalated.

"No one!" Barnes insisted.

"Yeah, right." Dave snorted. He leaned forward in an increasingly hostile pose. He can be a bit caveman at times. And not a Geico, go-bowling caveman, either.

I pressed a hand to his chest. "Honey, he might not be lying."

"Bullshit," Dave snapped.

I pushed harder to hold him in place. "Think about it, doofus! The camps are like Perez Hilton's damn blog. Gossip and rumors fly through there. If someone knew about the lab, especially people like the ones who hire us, we would have heard about it. Someone would have tried to use the information as leverage."

Dave's expression softened slightly. Caveman *could* be reasoned with, you see.

"Yeah, maybe," he grunted.

Barnes was nodding wildly. Apparently he didn't want any kind of escalation with my husband, either. "I knew I couldn't trust any of the ones who have brought me the heads with this secret. After spending just five minutes with most of them it was clear to me that none had the skills or the mind power to collect zombies themselves. I soon deduced they were all using your services to bring me what I desired."

"We were the middle man," I muttered with a shake of my head. "Son of a bitch."

"Just from hearing about you," the doctor continued, "and by observing you a few times from a safe distance, I could see you two were the clear leaders in killing zombies."

"So why not just call upon us out in the open?" I asked. "Why go through the whole ruse of calling us here for a job and then taking us hostage?"

Barnes nodded. "I would have treated you with more respect, not to mention skipped the rather expensive trouble of using one of those idiots to post the note to you at camp, had I not heard more than once about David's cynicism about… well, anything that implies hope. I had to assume you wouldn't come had I made my true intentions clear."

My husband and I both flinched. Apparently we'd been a bit transparent, even to the morons who hired us.

"You might be right about that," Dave admitted, full of Grumpy-Pants irritation.

"I thought the only way I had any chance of obtaining your assistance was to *show* you what I've done here. To prove to you through your own experiences that I wasn't a quack making false promises."

Dave nodded slowly. "I *guess* that makes sense. For a mad scientist."

Barnes exhaled a long breath. "If only I could test this serum on some human subjects, I would know for certain if it has the potential for curing these… *things*, or at least halting their desire to kill. And I'll also be able to see its effect on the human brain, which is considerably more complex than a rodent's."

"In most cases," I said with a faint smile.

Barnes laughed in response. It sounded rusty, but then I guess it was since he'd been alone for so long.

"True," the doctor said with a slight nod. "I must see if the brain is damaged irreparably by the full transformation."

"The guinea pigs seem okay," Dave muttered as we all looked at the cage.

"They're such simple creatures," Barnes sighed. "There is little difference in the behavior of one with brain damage and one without, I'm afraid." He turned his attention back to me. "In addition, I'd also like to be able to test my serum on subjects who have been bitten, but not fully transformed. That may be a way to stave off brain damage, but I'm not sure."

I nodded. I could see there were many variables to consider.

"Now, please," Barnes whispered, his gaze never leaving mine. "Will you help me? Will you save us all?"

"All right, all right," Dave said as he sat back down. "Let's not get overly dramatic."

"I don't think it's dramatic to—" the doctor began.

I could see this was going to get us nowhere except for the two idiots in the room with the penises acting like morons and bumping chests some more. So to nip that in the bud, I raised my hands.

"What's in it for us?"

Dave looked up at me in surprise and even Barnes stopped talking.

"I—well, you'd possibly be saving the world. I thought that might be enough compensation," Barnes said.

I snorted. "Oh, that's cute. How precious. Listen, Dr. Barnes—"

"Please, I'd like us to be friends. Call me Kevin."

I hesitated because his eyes were sparkling at me from behind his glasses and the Luke Wilson thing and the clean thing were a little mesmerizing.

"Kevin," I finally said. "The thing is, *Kevin*, you've been paying our little friends for what...a few weeks for work my husband and I have done. Saving the world is noble and all, but I'm with him." I jerked my thumb toward David. "I'll believe it when I see it. Until then, what's the deal?"

He nodded. "I do have military-grade weapons, as well as high-powered ammo that I'd be willing to exchange for your risk. In addition..." He trailed off and once again smiled at me. In fact, he hadn't looked at David for a few minutes. "Well, come with me and I'll show you something."

"His favorite thing to say," Dave said as he got up and motioned to the door. "Go ahead, Doc, lead. I can't wait to see what else you have besides infected guinea pigs and promises of a brave new world without zombies."

I gave him a look as the doctor led us to the door. We swooped down the hallways past more windows that looked into additional lab rooms. Many contained more guinea pigs, one had rows of heads in jars, apparently the fruits of our labor, but there were more than a few that had the shades drawn. Maybe they were sleeping quarters, I didn't know.

Barnes stopped at another door. This one wasn't locked like the others and it swung open when he pushed it. He smiled.

"Go ahead. *This* is what I offer to sweeten the deal for you, Sarah."

I wrinkled my brow as I passed into the darkened room. It was still and quiet, but then I noticed something. A steady sound I didn't recognize. At least, not at first.

Plink, plink, plink...

"Wait," I breathed as my mind adjusted to what it was processing. "Is that...is that..."

Behind me, Barnes...*Kevin*...flipped a light switch and the room was flooded with brightness. It was a bathroom. A clean, gloriously fresh bathroom. And the dripping was coming from a shower stall not three feet away from me.

I spun around and faced the two men at the door. My heart was racing and my mind spinning as I squealed, "Okay, we'll do it! We'll catch the zombies for you."

CHAPTER 6

Expand. Why stick to just killing zombies?
Or killing them just one way.

W e're equal partners, Dave," Dave said in the falsely high voice he always used to mimic me as he drove the van down the long, lonely highway. "We're in this together, Dave."

I blinked and tried to focus on his voice. It was hard to overcome the gloriousness of the fact that I was clean. *Really* clean. I smelled like soap and some kind of coconut shampoo and I kind of wanted to lick myself.

"Oh, come on," I said, dreamy as I pictured how the black sooty water had rinsed from my body and swirled around and around into the drain like it could wash away my sins and experiences over the past few months. "You *know* we were going to say yes to him in the end."

Dave glanced at me and muttered, "Well, maybe. Still, you can't just put us on the hook for something without talking it over with me first. We're supposed to be a team."

I gave him a little look. He didn't look mad, but

definitely a bit put out. Slowly, I edged a little closer to him and leaned over the gear shift between us.

"C'mon babe, admit that you like being all clean again."

"Hmph," was the response.

I moved closer and nuzzled his smooth neck. "*And* shaved."

"Hmmm," he said this time, though he sounded far less irritated than a moment before.

"And you *like* that I smell good."

Dave shrugged before he leaned down and pressed his freshly clean mouth to my sparkling mint one briefly.

"Fine," he said as he put his attention back on the road. "I admit it's a good trade. That *and* the weapons."

I glanced back. Yeah, we'd come out pretty well in our agreement with Barnes...*Kevin*. He'd handed over a stash of weaponry worthy of the most bad-ass zombie movie. We'd even gotten one of those handheld multi-shot cannons I'd coveted. I have to admit, I creamed my shorts a little every time I looked at it all awesome and deadly and stuff in the back of the van.

"We better find a place to hole up," Dave said, veering off the highway at an exit that said Moon Valley Country Club.

"True. We couldn't exactly go to the camps so clean and fresh, it would raise eyebrows," I said with a broad grin as he started scanning up and down the street for the perfect mansion for us to take over.

Like the whole car thing, the housing situation was another of the few fun elements to the apocalypse. Before the outbreak we lived in a shithole of a one-bedroom apartment.

Since then? Well, we'd lived it up in the ritziest resorts, fanciest suites, and the mansions of the ultra-rich and famous. I don't like to drop names but Paul McCartney has a ranch two and a half hours south of Phoenix. Just saying.

"You're right about not being able to go to camp like this," Dave said. "And I want to be able to talk freely about our plans anyway. If we're going to catch zombies, that's a whole other thing from blasting their brains out. I don't even have the first clue how to do it without getting killed...."

His voice trailed off as he pulled into a long, circular driveway that led up to a gorgeous mansion.

Tudor-style turrets lifted skyward and although the desert winds and heat had fried the grass and landscaping, there was nothing about the place that didn't scream "class."

Well, except for the ridiculous knight that was "standing guard" at the front door, rusting away from exposure to the elements.

Really, rich people? Really?

We got out, loading up on weapons before we made our way to the front door. Dave tested it and we both tensed when he found it was unlocked. Most of the time, houses like this got locked down tight the moment there was danger. The ritzy owners and spoiled dogs that lived there holed up to wait for help that never came. Or if they ran, they barred the doors behind them so that their precious stuff would be waiting for them when this mess was all over. They were oddly more afraid of looters than the living dead. Go figure.

So an open door at a house like this either meant that

the person within hadn't been *able* to lock the door…or someone else had gotten here first. Either way, it was a danger zone until we got it cleared.

We pushed our way into the house carefully. Outside the sun was setting and inside the rooms were dim and dusty. There was a faint smell of rotting food just in the foyer. The fridge had obviously been stocked when the shit went down. Hopefully so had the dry pantry so we could restock our tack box and even get some extra supplies for trade.

Dave's nose wrinkled at the gross smell as he gently shut the door behind us. "I forgot how much I missed electricity until that son of a bitch reminded me."

I smiled at the memory of real lights and hot, clean water, but quickly checked myself. Now wasn't the time for idle fantasies.

I grinned. "You *know* the fastest way to bring zombies so we can settle down for the night."

Dave shot me a glare and sighed. But he wasn't kidding anybody. He *liked* my games. "C'mon then and do it."

I pointed my shotgun at an angle toward the ceiling and pulled off a shot. A few feet away from us, plaster cracked and fell to the marble floor and the echoing sound of the shot made my ears ring. Acrid smoke filled my nose and the foyer.

"And *now* you smell like cordite," Dave pointed out as he swiped at the smoky air around us.

I frowned. Damn, he was right.

"I'll air out," I said as I stepped further into the foyer. "Hey, zombie assholes! Come and get it!"

Silence was the only response. I turned back around with a shake of my head. "I guess nobody's home."

"Shit!" he said. "Duck!"

After so many years together, and after so much time slaying zombies side by side, Dave and I sort of have a rapport. You know how it is . . . after enough time you start to "get" what a person is saying without having to clarify. So instead of asking for more info or turning to see what he was freaking out about, I dropped flat to my stomach on the marble floor.

The instant I was down, he pulled off a shot with his shotgun and then a second. My heart throbbed and my ears rang, but I couldn't get into shocked mode, I had to act. Keeping low, I flipped onto my back and lifted my shotgun. But there was nothing there.

"Clear?" I asked, my voice weak and soft from the ground.

"Clear," he panted.

I pushed up on my elbows and looked down the length of my body to see what he'd been shooting at. There, collapsed across the broken plaster I'd caused, were two zombies, a man and a woman. I got up, rubbing my elbow (I don't recommend dropping down on marble if you can avoid it, just an FYI) and looked at them.

The woman was wearing a fur coat. Not kidding. A fucking fur coat. Who even owned one of those in Arizona? Apparently this woman, though it was ill-fitting on her all-but-skeletal frame.

She also had on bunches of jewels. A ruby and diamond pendant, a big honking ring on each finger (all of which looked real, not costume) and the crowning glory were her earrings. Huge droplets of diamonds.

Unfortunately, their weight had tugged at her rotting ear lobes and now they were dragged almost to her shoulders like some native woman on a *National Geographic* special.

"I guess she must have put them all on to escape," Dave said with a shake of his head. "God, she's skinny."

I nodded. Here's a tidbit — most zombies are not thin. In fact, quite a few of them are fat fucks. I guess it comes from the never-ending food supply right outside their door. Also, I'm not sure how digestion of their prey works for them. If you know, don't tell me, I don't *want* to know.

But this lady, well, if she'd been anorexic in life, apparently she'd continued that trend in the unlife, too.

"What about the guy?" I said, turning my attention to the person half-hidden under fur-coat zombie.

"His clothes aren't so expensive," Dave said. "Maybe he was her butler."

I laughed at the mere idea of someone having a butler. Then again, it was a gloriously overpriced house before the zombies had significantly affected home values in the area. It's a bubble you just don't want to see burst, I promise you. It's waaaaay worse than subprime mortgages.

"Why the hell are they still in the house?" I asked as Dave kicked the front door open. We lifted the woman with effort and heaved her onto the drive. Tomorrow we'd kick her out of the way of the car, at least. Maybe.

He shrugged as we returned for the servant. "I have no idea. Most of them got a clue when they got turned and started out in the world looking for food. But this lady sure looks like she belongs here. Do you think she might have come home at night?"

"Like a homing pigeon?" I asked with a laugh. "They like to stay in one area, but I've never seen them actually come home. No, if this was her place, I'm guessing she never left after she turned."

We looked around the foyer, now damaged by my shot and the blood and sludge left over from the zombies.

"They were pretty crazed," Dave admitted. "I don't think I've ever seen any come so fast and look so hungry. Maybe they didn't know what to do to take care of themselves in life, so they just never figured it out in death, either."

"Either way, they're done now." I shut the door on our latest kills. "It's too bad we couldn't have caught them."

Dave looked at me sharply. "Yeah, they would have been perfect for your mad scientist. I bet he would have appreciated the fact that they were rich before they died."

I looked at him with a wrinkled brow. "You don't like the guy."

"No shit, Sherlock," he grunted.

I cocked my head. "But doesn't it excite you just a little that he maybe has a cure for all this?"

Dave shrugged. "I guess I just wonder what he was doing before he was so benevolently working on a cure. He seemed pretty ashamed...or at least unwilling to tell us when we asked him."

I stared at him. "We *all* have things we're not proud of from B.Z."

"B.Z.?" Dave sighed.

"Before Zombie," I said and he smiled despite himself. "Anyway, let's check out the rest of the house and then try to figure out how to catch a zombie for Kevin."

"Dr. Barnes," Dave corrected softly as he led the way to clear the house out. We'd learned the hard way to always check every room before declaring a place clean.

I followed him quietly, but in my head I corrected him back. *Kevin*.

CHAPTER 7

Profits are everything. But to get them
you have to catch a zombie.

Although our ideas for how to catch a zombie were
pretty much...um...*lame*, we still rolled out of the mansion the next day with an action item list. This was my
idea, of course, because I flipping love lists. Even in the
midst of zombie hell, I still made them and checked them
off. Dave shook his head at me, but whatever, I'm organized...bite me.

Unless you're a zombie. Then don't.

After a quick trip to the hardware store (with a *list* so
we wouldn't forget anything, thank you very much) we
were ready to try our hand at a new offshoot of the extermination game: animal (zombie?) control.

So here was our big plan, and yes, it is straight out
of the Wile E. Coyote playbook. Step one: obtain a net
(check!). Step two: set up net in a high-volume zombie
area. Step three: stand near the net to lure zombie/zom-
bies. Step four: trigger net and *voila*!

A zombie in a net.

Like I said, lame. But there's really no instruction manual on catching zombies (until we wrote one a few years later, but that's another story) and I still say it was better than the "dig a hole and cover it with sticks" idea we had discarded the night before.

What can I say? We were tired and apparently watched too many Looney Tunes as kids.

But now we stood in the parking lot of the once very high class and snooty Fashion Square Mall in Scottsdale. Well, *I* stood in the parking lot. Dave was up on the overhang that was part of the old entrance. He'd once been afraid of heights, but after months of running from monsters, old fears were sort of forgotten. Seriously, a zombie apocalypse is practically therapy for that petty shit.

Anyway, the overhang was made of a long, curved piece of steel and corrugated metal that was now covered in dirt and sand which obscured the sign that said SCOTTSDALE on the wall above it. The doors below, which led into the main mall, were once made of glass but had long ago been broken by zombies, looters, and people just trying to find a place to hide or sleep in this new world order.

Two marquis stores buffered the entrance. A Nordstrom (where that rich zombie woman from the mansion the night before once shopped, no doubt) and possibly a Crate and Barrel, although I couldn't tell because all the letters on the sign had crashed to the ground during the bombings and now the shell of the building was only left with a capital *C*, two of the letter *a*, and one lowercase *r* to identify it.

"You know, I think I'd shop at a store called Ca-ar!" I shouted up to David. "What do you think it would sell?"

He shot me a look over the ledge. "Sarah—"

"Something Norwegian, I bet," I continued.

"Sarah..." His tone was a mixture of annoyance and amusement.

"Like Ikea."

He leaned a little further over the ledge and his glare silenced me. "You know, just because I can manage heights now, doesn't mean I like them. *Stop distracting me.*"

I shook my head, but obeyed. I had to focus while I made another patrol scan all around the area anyway. The mall itself was half-collapsed, so I wasn't too worried about it, especially since the last half an hour of our being here shouting at each other hadn't brought out any zombie mall-walking groups looking for an easy meal.

Behind me, a few zombies roamed at the edge of the deserted parking lots. Most of them hadn't seen us yet (their eyesight, not so good. Must have to do with the rotting), but when I checked through my rifle scope it seemed like one or two were shambling toward us rather than aimlessly in circles. I could only hope we'd get set up before they came roaring into our space. If we weren't, we'd have to kill them and the noise and distraction of that would probably bring more coming.

It would be a pain in the ass if nothing else. Really, the best scenario was if we could just get one or two zombies coming at us rather than a crowd.

But that didn't happen very often.

"Okay," Dave said as he scootched to the edge of the awning and swung himself down onto the roof of the van. "I think we're all ready up there."

After he joined me on the ground, we backed up and

looked at our handiwork. I'd love to say it was a really well put-together thing, destined to become the gold standard for this shit, but it wasn't. The whole system was pretty shabby, but it was what we had.

I sighed. "So basically I'm going to try to get one of them to stand on the net and then you're going to drop the weight and pull them up over the pulley system you created with that tree and the awning."

He nodded without looking away from the trap. "You're right except that *I'm* going to lure the zombie and *you're* going to launch the pulley."

I turned toward him. "What? No way!"

He grunted in that non-committal caveman way. Okay, so David can be a little protective of me. Even now when he knows I've got the chops for zombie killing, he still tries to shelter me. I love the guy for it, but it drives me nuts, too.

"There's only one way to solve this," I said with a sigh as I held out my fist toward him. "Rock-Paper-Scissors."

"You want to Rock-Paper-Scissors for your life?" he asked after a slight pause.

I nodded. "We've done it for worse."

"Oh. My. God," he began, but I shook my head.

"No arguing. Time's a-wastin' and zombies are a-comin'. Now let's go, best two out of three."

Ten minutes later, Dave was back up on the roof and I was standing beside the net, staring up at him as I shielded my eyes from the bright sun.

"So I'm just going to try to loop one in, okay?"

He nodded. "I've got my rifle ready though, just in case you need coverage." He hesitated. "Good luck. Be careful."

I gave him a little wave. "Thanks, babe."

With a deep breath, I turned back toward the parking lot. Now I just needed a zombie. Surprisingly, *a* zombie was going to be the hard part.

I stared out across the big lot. The slowly shambling zombies were still, well, shambling, but they were still too far away to get to them without attracting the attention of the five or ten more just aimlessly staggering around farther out.

I set my rifle down so it wouldn't weigh me down when I had to run and checked in my waistband to be sure my 9mm was still there. The knife in the sheath at my thigh would also have to do, though I hated the idea of a close-quarters fight with one of the infected.

With that done, I started walking around the perimeter of the mall. And to draw the attention of any zombie/zombies lurking around without making *too* much noise, I began to whistle. First I whistled a little Killers, then some Bon Jovi, but it wasn't until I moved on to 50 Cent's "In Da Club" that I heard a faint rustling in some overgrown desert shrubbery around the corner from the mall entrance.

"More of a hip-hop fan, eh?" I asked as I edged closer. "C'mon, little guy. C'mon out and let Auntie Sarah have a look at you."

I asked for it. With a wet, hollow grunt, a zombie burst from the bushes. He was holding a human hand in his teeth like a dog and I flinched. I guess we'd been too late to help his latest victim.

As the hand dropped from his mouth, he looked at me and I stared at him. He was no "little guy." This guy had been *big* in the world before infection. Maybe even a bodybuilder or something. He was tall and broad-shouldered and once his chest had probably rippled with muscle.

I say *once* because the thing about death is that your muscles and tissues break down. This is true for zombies, too (though they do seem to top out on rotting after a week or ten days — again, don't know why and please don't tell me). With this guy, the decomposition had resulted in his muscle fibers drooping and pulling until they ripped away from the bones. Now they hung from gooey, fleshy hunks of meat like an ill-fitting shirt.

"Oh, buddy," I said with a cluck of my tongue. "Not a good look for you."

The zombie tilted his head with a questioning whine and smelled the air like they sometimes do. His rotting lips spread tightly against his teeth and he let out another groaning wail.

"Well come on!" I said, using a voice like I'd use with a puppy or a toddler as I started backing toward the front of the mall. "Come and get me."

I didn't have to ask twice. The zombie lurched out of the bushes, oblivious to the fact that some of the hard, dead branches had stuck in his legs and now tore loose and stayed in his flesh like weird porcupine quills as he walked. If it wasn't so gross, it would have been pretty comical.

At first his movements were slow, but as I got further out of his reach, his hunter instinct kicked in and he began a herky-jerky jog.

That was it, all I needed to get my ass moving. I took off toward the front entrance, shouting, "I've got one!"

As I careened around the corner, I looked up. Dave was

standing on the awning, one hand on the pulley mechanism to launch the net up around the zombie and one hand balancing the shotgun against his thigh, ready to take the shot if I needed him.

"Fuck, he's a big boy!" Dave screamed back down at me.

I jogged toward the netting, and only once I reached it did I flip around so I faced my quarry again. He was pretty fast for such a big dude and was already just fifteen feet away.

"Get ready!" I urged.

"I'm on it," came the reply from above in Dave's most tense voice. He was *not* happy about this and I knew it.

But it didn't matter, at least not for now. As I waited for the zombie, barely inching back to entice him with little shuffles, the big lug stepped onto the net.

"Now!" I screamed.

Up above I heard Dave doing something, but the net didn't budge. It didn't move even as the goliath of a zombie strode toward me like fucking Godzilla to my helpless Japanese city.

"Any time, dear," I cried, my wide eyes glued on the monstrosity reaching for me straight out of some 1930s horror movie.

"I triggered it and—"

Dave hadn't finished the sentence when the big infected creature stepped off of the net. The moment he was clear, the pulley system whizzed into life and lifted up to catch nothing but air. It kind of reminded me of those arcade claw machine things with the cheap stuffed animals I'd tried to win as a kid. Only I didn't *die* when I didn't get one.

"Shit, there's a delay in the mechanism," he called down.

"You think?" I called back as I started to run again. "Reset and I'll try to bring him around for a second pass."

I jerked from one side to the other as I tried to determine the best way to go. I was pretty sure I could get the big brainless monster to follow me, then all I had to do was make a big circle in the parking lot until Dave was reset and we'd try another—

Before I could finish the thought there was a wet thunk and suddenly the blade of a machete stuck out of the zombie's head right between his eyes.

The massive bastard teetered for a moment, his rotting eyebrows knitted together like he had a question on the tip of his tongue, then he collapsed forward on his knees and finally face planted on the drive, his skull almost cleaved in half from Dave's blade.

I stared at his dead body for a long moment, almost in disbelief. Then I slowly lifted my gaze to the awning. Dave stood on the edge, his rifle trained on the dead body before me.

"What the hell?" I called up as he turned the weapon away from me. "*What the hell*, David?"

He shrugged and looked anything but apologetic. "Look, it didn't work and until I figure out the timing on the pulley, I won't take the risk with your life that he'd catch you while you were running."

"Shit, David, I could have jogged that prick around the lot for the whole day and kept trying to catch him."

I threw up my hands and kicked the zombie to expel some of my frustration. My boot hit soft flesh with a sickening thunk. Great, now I had mung on my boots and even though that was my own fault, I'd decided to blame David for it, too.

My husband turned his face. "Yeah, and eventually the living dead coming over here from the edge of the parking lot would have reached us and then what?"

I stomped my foot (spraying ick on the pavement around me) and clenched my fists straight down at my sides.

"Well, first, the ones out there are lurching, not running, and you *know* they wouldn't have started running until they could smell me, which would have taken half an hour at least. And when that happened, *then* you could have killed some of them. But shit, man, at least give the plan a chance. We're never going to catch one if you give up and start throwing machetes the second a zombie looks at me cross-eyed."

"I'm not even sure fucking catching these freaks is a smart idea," he said with a deepening frown. "Is it really worth the risk?"

"Christ, stop being such a girl!" I snapped. "I mean, we could really *do* something and you're ninnying around!"

There was a long silence from above and then Dave softly said, "Well, excuse me for trying to look after you."

That shut me up. For a long moment we just looked at each other, kind of like the big zombie and I had around the corner. But this stare was waaaay more uncomfortable. Finally, he turned away.

"I'll reset the pulley. From what I saw, I *think* I might have figured out the timing on it."

I nodded as I turned back toward the parking lot with

a sigh. I didn't like fighting. We'd done enough of that in our life B.Z.

I guess I should have apologized or maybe gone up on the roof to talk it out with him, but before I could make any decisions about my husband, I saw something off in the distance that caught my eye. A flash of movement that was too quick and certain to be from a zombie.

I dropped down to grab my rifle and leaned it across my lap as I stared through the scope. I scanned the distance for the movement again and when I found it I nearly fell over.

"Holy shit!" I cried as I staggered to my feet. "Reset it, reset it!"

"I *am*," Dave grunted from above. "Almost done, what's your rush?"

"There's a kid!" I cried as I trained my rifle on the scene unfolding across the lot. "And he's got zombies on his tail."

"What?" Dave asked as the netting dropped back on the pavement. He lifted his own gun and stared at the lot.

We both watched as the kid, maybe about ten or twelve — it was hard to tell from this distance — sprinted through the lot toward us. Behind him were two zombies, doing that run that is so Goddamned disturbing, no matter how much time has gone by and no matter how many times you see it. Seriously, the dead shouldn't jog.

Although, to be fair, before all this started I was of the belief that *I* should never jog either unless something was chasing me.

So then things started chasing me.

But I digress. The poor kid was pretty athletic, actually.

The zombies were still at an impressive distance behind him and he wasn't allowing them to catch up.

"I've got the lead in my sights," Dave said from above. "I'm taking the shot."

I nodded and watched in my own scope as the explosive sound of my husband's gun firing was quickly followed by the lead zombie behind the little boy dropping to the ground in a pile of brains and blood.

The child jerked a little in surprise, but quickly turned toward us. Smart kid, running toward the people who were your saviors. Trust me, in a post-zombie world, that didn't always happen. People were a bit "Mad Max" at this point, a little wary of others who didn't come from their own tribe or camp.

"I don't have a clear shot of the one behind," Dave said as he slid the action on his rifle. I heard the plunk of the empty shell hitting the mall roof.

"Just wait…" I said, hardly able to catch my breath from the excitement. "I can get him, but maybe we can use the kid to catch him instead."

Dave jerked as he looked down at me. "Are you nuts?"

"Look, he's perfect," I said as I stared through the sight again. "Not too big, not too small—"

"Are you talking about the zombie or the *terrified child*?"

I ignored Dave's outrage, too focused on the idea of capturing a monster to listen to him.

"Grab the rope, they're almost here." I moved behind the net and motioned to the kid. "Come on! Come right to me!"

The little boy didn't need to be told twice. He rushed

toward me and it was only from the closer distance that I noticed he was carrying a cute little .38 Special, just like a boy playing cowboys and Indians. Only I had a hunch his weapon was real and the zombie wasn't playing.

"Shoot him, stupid!" the child screamed as he ran past me.

I readied my rifle to do just that, but as the zombie approached, his gaping mouth biting and his hands clawing, this time Dave's timing was perfect. The net slung up under the rotting living corpse and sent him flying up in the air, his arms and legs akimbo as the trap closed around him and left him dangling from the awning.

The little boy and I stood below him, looking up as he clawed at the netting, chewing at the rope and snarling and spitting down at us. I tilted my head as I examined him closer. Was that a damn mohawk? Sheesh, kids these days.

"Why the *fuck* didn't you shoot him?" the child finally said, and suddenly the little pissant was slapping at my arms, pummeling me with his tiny fists.

"Hey!" I cried as I slapped back out of instinct. I might have been a zombie killer, but our hands smacked like two stupid girls fighting over a washed-up singer on a reality show. "Why didn't *you*? You had a gun!"

The little boy stopped slapping me and tossed the pistol aside. "Mine's empty, dummy. Like your head. What, did the zombies already get to you, dumbass?"

"Ha, ha," I said with a sneer.

Dave climbed down onto the van and jumped to the ground between us. "Okay, children, enough. Sorry we didn't shoot, kid, but we were trying to catch this fucker."

The little boy glared at us again, but this time his

expression said he thought we were cuckoo. Not that I blamed him really, although I was still thrilled to look up and see a zombie swinging from the overhang.

"Catch one? You two are crazy."

"That's probably an understatement," I said with a grin for David.

The little boy didn't smile back. Instead, he reared back and kicked me straight in the shin with all his might.

"You still should have shot it."

And *that* was how we met Robbie, otherwise known as "The Kid."

CHAPTER 8

Don't forget the little people.
Even when you want to.

The Kid reminded me of Bart Simpson. He had blond hair that was probably once lovingly combed into place for school pictures by his mom, but apparently he'd been left to his own devices for a while now because it was currently spiked up from dirt and not enough personal grooming. Oh, and he kept going on about a skateboard, which was apparently his major mode of transportation until it got broken by the same zombies who were chasing him across the parking lot.

Not to mention, he was kind of a little punk, as my bruised shin was throbbing testament to.

I glared at him as he sat in his place on the curb in front of the mall. He was eating some kind of no-name snack cake, his grubby little gross fingers leaving chocolaty smears around his mouth.

"So...now we have him," Dave said with a heavy sigh. "What do you want to *do* with him?"

I glared at The Kid. "Kick him back when he's not ready for it."

Dave stared at me for a long moment and then slowly extended his finger (I won't say which one, you can guess) upward toward the net that swung above us in the breeze.

"I meant what do you want to do about *that*?"

I shook my head and looked up. The creature was still thrashing around and growling at us, but apparently the infected don't have much stamina (or maybe this particular one just didn't have any in life or something) because his movements had become more sluggish and his growls less aggressive and harsh. Poor little guy was just getting tuckered out.

"We have to get him down, I guess," I said.

The Kid snorted from behind us and both of us turned to stare at him. He smirked as he wiped his dirty hands on what had once been pale blue jeans and said, "You're *really* smart, right?"

I've never wanted to strike a child as much as I did at that moment. I probably would have, too, but Dave caught my arm and held me in place.

"Sarah," he said low and near my ear.

"Look, *Robbie*," I said, using the name The Kid had given us when we demanded an introduction after he kicked the hell out of my leg. "You're just a little brat, okay, so don't pretend you know something about catching zombies that we don't. Why don't you run along?"

"Sarah!" David gasped in disbelief. When I looked at him he shook his head. "You really want to send the kid off on his own, unarmed in an apocalypse? What is he, ten?"

"I'm almost twelve, actually," The Kid interjected with

a been-there-done-that look. "Or I will be in six months. And I *don't* need your help."

"You needed it a minute ago," I said, barely resisting the urge to stick my tongue out at him.

He shrugged. "I guess, but just so you know, I would have figured it out even if I *hadn't* seen you two."

I stared at him. He was an annoying little twerp, but you couldn't help but be impressed by him. After all, he wasn't even a teen and was apparently alone after three months of zombie un-awesomeness. So he was probably right he would have figured it out.

I returned my attention to the swinging zombie pendulum above us since anything I had to say to The Kid at that point wouldn't have been particularly useful.

"We can lower him to the ground pretty easily with the pulley system," I said as I stared again at our prey. "But then how do we secure him? He'll thrash all over the place in the back of the van. And if he got loose..."

I shuddered at the thought of being trapped in such a small space with a zombie.

Dave was silent as he pondered that, but before he could give me his answer, The Kid piped up again. "You could lower him halfway and then use a rope to tie him tighter. You two geniuses *do* have a rope, don't you?"

"Yes, we have a fucking rope," I said through clenched teeth.

The Kid shrugged. "Well, it would be easy. Just spin him like a piñata."

I stared, partly because it was a pretty good plan and partly because the kid's mouth was full of something. Again.

"Where are you getting so much food?" I asked as I

watched him pop a Starburst into his mouth and toss the wrappers at his feet.

Without blinking, he pointed to his cargo jean pockets.

"Those are bad for your teeth," I snapped, even though I had to admit I wanted one myself. But I wasn't about to ask *him* to share. I shook my head and returned my attention to David. "What do you think? Would that work?"

My husband nodded. "It's probably our best bet. And maybe we can use one of those burlap sacks from the old head-collecting days to cover his head and tie it, too. Less chance for grazing bites."

"Alrighty," I agreed.

"Do I get a cut?" The Kid asked as we started back toward the van so Dave could climb up on the awning and run the pulley system and I could grab the rope from one of our color-coordinated storage containers.

I stared at The Kid in confusion. "What?"

"Look, I'm not stupid just because I'm younger than you," the little boy said as he folded his arms and stared at me with the most jaded expression I'd ever seen. Even Dave couldn't have topped this one. "If you two are going to this much trouble to catch a zombie, rather than exterminate it like your stupid van says, my bet is you're going to get paid for it, right? So do I get a cut?"

Dave snorted out a laugh as he started to climb up onto the van. "Don't kill him, Sarah," he called back to me.

I decided not to deny what The Kid was saying because it would just take too long. "What do you mean, do you get a cut? Why would *you* get a cut?"

"It's *my* zombie you caught."

I stared. "What do you mean *your* zombie? It was chasing you, it wasn't your pet."

He ignored me. "*And* it's my idea that you're using to tie it up. So I should get a cut."

I shut my eyes and slowly counted to ten in my head as I tried desperately to remember that this was a child who was probably pretty traumatized by everything he had seen and done in the months since the outbreak. But when I looked at him again, all I saw was brat. And snot-nosed brat at that. Gross.

"No way," I sneered.

The Kid got to his feet, sending empty candy wrappers to blow away on the breeze as he folded his arms. "Yes way."

Above us, Dave sighed. "Am I going to have to separate you two?"

I glanced up at him. Although he had a joking tone to this voice, his face was tired. I frowned. Clearly I was creating more stress for him than he needed and over what? Some bratty little kid who would be gone from our lives before sundown. It wasn't worth it.

Without another word, I turned my back to him and grabbed a long coil of rope from the back of the van. Positioning myself near the thrashing zombie, I gave David the thumbs-up signal.

"Ready!"

With the dead weight of the zombie in the net, Dave had to work a little harder to ease the netting down toward me slowly, but after a lot of grunting and swearing, he had gotten the net even with me, but still slightly off the ground.

The zombie hissed and growled at me, pressing his face against the net so hard that the fabric bit into his rotting flesh and left raw hash marks across his cheeks and lips that would never heal.

"Settle down, buddy," I said as I tried to catch his

lurching form to start the rope around him. He kept moving and flinching though, so I couldn't tie him up.

"Fuck!" I said as he gave me the slip another time. "I need another set of hands."

Dave stared at me and I stared up at him for a minute before both of us slowly turned toward The Kid.

He had moved to the front of the van and was now leaning on it nonchalantly, one ankle crossed over the other. He smiled as I looked at him.

"What's my cut?" he asked, enunciating each word with a smug smile.

I shook my head. *This* was why I didn't have kids. Finally I growled, "You can have twenty percent of whatever we get for the zombie."

"Fifty," the kid snorted.

Dave's cackle of laughter was the answer. "No way. We caught it, we're driving it and loading and unloading it. Twenty-five."

"Thirty," The Kid said without even hesitating or blinking. "And ammo."

I bit my lip and nodded. "Fine. Now come here and help me."

To his credit, once the deal had been made, The Kid hopped to it. He ran over, dodging the straining, clawing fingers and gnashing teeth of the zombie, and grabbed one end of the rope.

"Okay, first we need to pull his arms tight," I said. "And then wrap him up with the rest of the rope and tie it off."

To my surprise, there was no debate or argument from The Kid. He just swept his side of the rope around the infected creature in the net and we hurried to wrap the rope around him so that his arms were now fully bound at his sides. Around and around we went, trading sides to bind the creature up until he was bound like an old-fashioned play about a girl tied to a railroad track by Snidely Whiplash. *Mwahahaha...*

"That looks good, now tie him off," Dave called from above as we swept the rope around the zombie a final time.

By now he was squirming like an angry caterpillar forced into a cocoon. He still snapped at us through the rope, black sludge pouring from his gray lips as he gnawed at the netting.

I took the other side of the rope from The Kid and started to work on knotting the ends together, but I didn't make much progress before he let out a sigh and snatched them away from me.

"Jeez, lady," he said as he gave me a 'You-Are-A-Stupid-Adult' look. "Learn to tie a knot, why don't you?"

I watched as he crossed and recrossed the rope a few times and finally came out with the tightest, most complicated knot I'd ever seen.

"Where did you learn to do *that*?" I asked, sort of stunned into grudging respect as I tugged at the knot and it didn't give even a fraction.

He shrugged. "I was in Boy Scouts before—"

He cut himself off and turned away. It was one of the few times I saw The Kid really look like he felt anything bad about the apocalypse. Like all of us, he had a coping mechanism for forgetting life Before Zombies. The little reminder of a Boy Scout knot made him more like a kid again to me. I almost felt sorry for him.

Almost.

"Hey," I said softly. "I'm going to put the sack over

his head. Do you think you could use one of those super knots to tie it off around his neck, too?"

He nodded and when he looked at me again any regret or childlike heartbreak I'd seen in his face was gone. Jaded Kid was back.

"Whatever."

I stifled a smile as I returned to the back of the van and grabbed a burlap sack. It would hold a zombie head like it had so many times before ... only this time it would be one attached to a body.

When I returned to the netted infected I looked at him. There wasn't an obvious way to get the sack over his face now that I considered it. The net drew shut above him, which meant you couldn't really pull something over top of his rotting skull. There was no choice to it, I was going to have to free his head.

I withdrew my knife from the sheath at my thigh and carefully cut one or two of the net's ropes. I didn't want to do too much in case we wanted to use this netting method again, but just enough to give the zombie space to push his head out. It didn't take long before he realized he could do just that. Straining against the binds, he shoved his head through the spot and resumed biting in my general direction. His teeth, grey from rot and stained from sludge, snapped as they gnashed together, grinding with the anticipation of devouring human flesh and blood.

"Sarah!" Dave called from above. "What the hell, you're cutting up the net?"

I shrugged. "I need to get to him. I'll repair it later. Now can you lower him a bit more?"

Dave muttered something from above but the zombie dropped a little lower just as I'd asked. Now his shaking, twisting head was even with my chest and he stared at my tits. Before the outbreak, I'd had guys do this too, but for this guy they were more of a meal than a toy, no matter how cute I knew I looked in my black tank top with the little hint of lace from the bra peeking out beneath it. I ignored his snarls as I lined up the sack and then yanked it over his head.

And now I knew what riding a bull felt like. The zombie started to jerk, turning toward me, straining against the burlap until I could see his angry face outlined against the tight fabric.

"Robbie?" I said with effort as I rolled and rocked along with the creature's jerking motions. Eight seconds, right? Well, I'm sure I beat that and then some, but will they make a movie starring me? Hmph.

The Kid rushed forward and wrapped the rope around the zombie's neck.

"Pull tight," I suggested as he started to tie off the rope that now caused the skin around the infected's neck to bulge. "It's not like you can kill him."

The Kid chuckled and finished his knot. As soon as he was done and I'd let go, Dave released his hold on the rope and the zombie slid down to the ground with a loud, cracking thud. We all winced even though you couldn't exactly feel *sorry* for the thing. Even if you broke all his bones, he'd still drag himself along to eat you.

Plenty of people had gotten turned by broken and busted-up infected friends and family members. After a while you sort of got immune to their injuries, mainly because they never stopped coming for you until you took their heads.

"Well," I sighed as Dave came back down from the

awning for the third time. He was getting so comfortable at doing it, I wondered if he even noticed the height thing anymore. "That was some good teamwork. Now, thanks a lot, Kid, but we—"

"No, no, no," The Kid interrupted as he stomped toward me with his little fists raised in a fighting stance. A pretty good one, too. He was future UFC material with that form. "No way are you fucking me out of my pay."

"Hey!" I snapped. "Language."

He shot me a look that could have killed. "Screw you, lady. You owe me a third of whatever you get plus ammo."

"And we're going to give you that, Robbie," Dave said, his tone so much more adult and soothing than mine.

Funny, I used to get so pissed because I felt like Dave was stuck in adolescence, but now ... well, he wasn't that guy on the couch playing video games instead of getting a job anymore.

I dropped my own tone to match his, hoping, I guess, to impress him a little. "Seriously, Kid. We're not going to fuck you over. We're *more* than happy to give you supplies equal to thirty percent of what we're paid for this job and the ammo right now and you can be on your way."

The Kid folded his arms. "Oh yeah, right. Like I'm going to just believe that whatever you give me is thirty percent. No way. I'm coming with you to wherever you're going and I'm watching you get your payment. *Then* we'll decide together what thirty percent amounts to."

I gave Dave a side glance. I'm sure that would really impress Dr. Barnes ... *Kevin* ... when we revealed that we had not only brought in another person on our scheme, but that he wasn't even in puberty yet. I hated to think of his reaction.

"I don't know," Dave said with a shake of his head. "That may not go over. This is sort of top-secret stuff."

The Kid snorted. "Okay, Mr. and Mrs. CIA. If it was so secret, you never should have let me help you in the first place."

I opened my mouth to point out, once again, that we hadn't invited him to help us do anything, but he kept talking.

"But you did, so a deal is a deal. I'm going with you."

I glared at the boy, then waved David over to the side for a confab. "What do we do?" I whispered. "He can't come to the warehouse."

Dave shot him a look over my shoulder. "I think there's not much choice. I mean, you can't really blame him for doubting our intentions. And he *did* help us out."

"Barnes is going to think we're a bunch of idiots," I moaned.

Dave rolled his eyes. "I'm sure your boyfriend will get over it."

"Haha," I sneered as he turned away and faced The Kid again.

"Okay, look, you can come with us." Dave hesitated. "But when we get close to where we're going, we'll have to blindfold you so you can't see."

The Kid's brow wrinkled and there was a moment of nervous hesitation on his face that made him look as young as his years. Then he shook it off.

"Okay, I guess. But if you go all Catholic Priest on me, I'll cut your hands off."

Dave stared at him. "Gross. On both accounts. Trust me, I've no interest in going anything *on* you. I just want to make sure you're not going to interfere and cause trouble with our contact. If you come, you keep your mouth shut, got it?" Dave asked in a stern and sort of fatherly tone.

The Kid stared at him for a long moment where I swear he actually looked a little impressed. So was I, truth be told. Then he nodded. "Okay."

"Now let's load this fucker up and get going. Thanks to all our noise those ones on the outskirts are getting too close for comfort and I'm just not in the mood for a showdown," Dave said as he grabbed for our captured zombie's feet and motioned me to take the shoulder area to toss him in the back of the van.

CHAPTER 9

Strive for more. More zombies,
more fighting, more profit...

It took us a while to get rolling and then there was all the drama of blindfolding Robbie to deal with, too. The Kid was such a *whiner*, you'd think we were burning his eyes out with acid, not gently wrapping them with an old neck-tie Dave had in the van. I don't know why he had one. It wasn't like we were going out on job interviews or to a fancy restaurant any time soon.

Anyway, by the time we actually got back to the warehouse it was almost dark.

Dark was bad. Always. We had to hurry.

Dave killed the engine and we sat there for a minute, looking up at the ramshackle building that hid so much.

With a heavy breath that told me how little he was looking forward to this, he reached back and tugged The Kid's blindfold down around his neck.

"We're here," he said.

The Kid blinked a few times and then leaned forward from his place crouched on the back floor next to our writhing captive. He looked out the front windshield and wrinkled his nose in contempt.

"You should have gotten paid up front. This is a dump."

"Looks can be deceiving," Dave said as he got out and started around to the back of the van to pull our quarry out for delivery.

I grinned as I opened my own door. "Yeah. I mean, *you* look like a nice little boy at first glance. But we all know that's bullshit."

The Kid stuck his tongue out as I got out. When I reached the back of the van he had gotten himself behind our zombie and was helping push as Dave hauled him out.

I jumped into the fray. With a lot of grunting and swearing, we managed to finally lift the writhing body from the back. I had its shoulders and Dave the kicking, flailing feet. The thing was dead weight, but dead weight that kept fighting and growling. I would *not* be sorry to see it go.

I looked up at the building as I shifted my part of the load. "Think he's watching?"

Dave nodded. "Hell yeah. He's probably on his way up to—"

Before he could finish, the broken door opened and Barnes rushed out much like he had the day before. Only this time there were no readied weapons or threats. This time he had a grin on his surprisingly handsome geeky face and he clapped his hands together as he approached us.

"That's it, isn't it?" he gushed as he looked at the moving bundle of rope and burlap in our arms. "It's perfect. Just beautiful."

I sniffed as I looked at our bundle. It was oozing. Apparently Kevin had some fucked-up ideals when it came to beauty.

"Come, come inside," he encouraged us as he backed toward the warehouse. "Bring it here."

We followed him into the building, our arms heavy with our squirming bundle and with The Kid a few steps behind us. Kevin was so wrapped up in our gift for him that he didn't even seem to notice we had an extra crew member. That is, until we reached the hidden elevator shaft. After Kevin had hit the button opening the floor, only then did he look back and his broad smile fell.

"What is *that*?" he asked, his nostrils flaring as he pointed across the empty expanse toward The Kid.

I chuckled. "He claims to be a child."

Dave shot me a dirty look as we shifted the load. The zombie started to moan and groan louder and louder and he had to almost shout as he explained, "This is Robbie. He...um...*helped* us while we were working on capturing the zombie."

"You needed assistance from a child?" Kevin asked with an arched brow. He kept his gaze firmly on David, almost as if he put the majority of the blame on him.

"I'm not a child, I'm almost twelve," The Kid snapped. Both Dave and I shot him a "shut-the-hell-up" glare like my mom used to give me in church about a hundred years ago.

I wished I could step closer to Kevin, but with the zombie in our arms, it wasn't possible. Instead, I shifted the load (my shoulders were starting to fucking *kill* me).

"The Kid sort of inserted himself into the issue. We didn't invite him," I explained. "Anyway, it doesn't matter, does it? We got the zombie."

"You did, indeed," Kevin said with a broad smile for me.

I heard Dave's soft but highly irritated sigh beside me. "Look, asshat, this thing is really getting heavy. If you don't mind..."

He nudged his head toward the elevator.

Kevin jerked, almost as if no one had ever called him a name before. But I guess if you were a highly educated doctor who spent his time doing research under an abandoned warehouse...maybe no one had. At least not since high school.

"O-of course," he said as he stepped back and let us— *all* of us, including The Kid—onto the lift panel.

We rode down in an awkward silence. Dave and I kept shifting as our zombie jerked in our arms, The Kid was sulking about being called a child, and Barnes was just staring at our captive in pure rapture.

In fact, the only noise as we moved from the red to the green to the bright white lights were the groaning whines of our little zombie friend. And even they were getting softer.

The doors dinged open and into the bright light of the sterile hallways we moved. Of course, The Kid hadn't ever been here before, so I couldn't help but shoot a quick look behind at him to see his reaction.

Even *he* couldn't be jaded about this. He was still standing in the elevator shaft, his eyes wide as saucers as he stared at the hallway. I smiled. He looked like an eleven-year-old at that moment, only instead of being impressed by a toy store, it was light and cleanliness that blew his mind.

"Follow me," Kevin said as he moved down the hallway.

After a few awkward turns, he unlocked one of the little

lab rooms where the shades were drawn so you couldn't see inside. Barnes motioned us past him, flattening against the wall as we passed so the zombie wouldn't touch him.

There was a table in the middle of the room with restraints across it. Dave shot me a quick glance as we set the thrashing zombie down on it. I ignored it.

"Want us to strap him down?" I asked as I turned back to the doctor.

He shook his head. "No, no. I'll set him up myself."

He motioned us from the room and shut the door behind us. I heard the lock click back into place.

"Most excellent work, Sarah. You have impressed me beyond measure, and trust me I had extremely high hopes for you," Kevin began, reaching out to take my hand.

When he saw it was covered in blood and sludge from our little zombie friend, he hesitated and instead slid his fingers up to my bare bicep. He squeezed gently there, his fingers surprisingly soft. I guess I was used to rough hands like Dave's.

I stared at the hand on my arm for a moment and then smiled.

"Well, it was truly a team effort," I said as I looked at Dave. He was also staring at Kevin's hand on my bare arm. "Right, honey?"

He continued to stare a moment longer and then grunted. "Go Team," he muttered, the sarcasm dripping from his tone like poison. "So we'd like to get paid, thanks."

Kevin flinched and I did, too. It seemed so gauche to talk about payment when the doctor was busy congratulating us. Or congratulating *me*, anyway, since Dave hardly seemed to register with him unless he was annoyed. But the discomfort cleared from his face instantly and he released my arm as he turned toward Dave.

"Of course. Please feel free to use the shower facilities at your leisure. And I have put a store of additional weaponry and ammunition on a wheeled cart near the elevator. I think you'll find them more than satisfactory compensation." His smile returned to me. "And Sarah, I hung some new clothing for you in the bathroom stall behind the door. I hope that isn't too forward."

Dave sucked in a sharp breath but before he could answer the question directed toward me, I jumped in front of him. "Well, thank you, Dr. Barnes—"

He shot me a look and I smiled.

"*Kevin*," I corrected myself, swiftly, even as I reached back and patted Dave's hand since I could *feel* his temper bubbling silently. "I'll certainly take whatever you found for me, but I'm happy to bring my own fresh clothes in."

"Of course." Kevin looked sheepish as he shoved his glasses up his nose nervously. "I overstepped, and I apologize. Next time—"

"Wait," Dave interrupted, shaking off my hand which was still patting him and coming around to stand next to me. "*Next time*? What the fuck do you mean, *next time*?"

Kevin stared at Dave for a long moment and then he shook his head. "I'm afraid I don't understand the question."

Dave clenched his fists and his voice strained through obviously clenched teeth. "You said you wanted a Goddamned zombie to run your little experiments on. So *we* brought you a Goddamned zombie. That's it. That was the deal. So what the hell do you mean fucking *next time*?"

Kevin looked at me, then Dave, then back at me. "I'm

sorry if I wasn't clear. I thought you understood. I'll need far more than one specimen to do a truly useful test of my curative serum. There are variables to be dealt with and overcome. The more zombies you can bring me, the better."

My insides clenched as Dave stared at the doctor.

"Getting *one* was almost suicide," Dave said. His voice was quiet now but that didn't mean he wasn't angry. In fact, Quiet Dave was an infinitely more Dangerous Dave. "And now you want *more*?"

"That's stupid," The Kid agreed from behind us and all of us jumped.

He'd been so quiet since we reached the lab, I think we'd all forgotten about him (it didn't happen often, I assure you). Now I shot him another church glare. He wasn't making the situation better by encouraging Dave's anger and resistance to what Kevin wanted from us.

I grabbed Dave's arm and held tight. Reluctantly he stopped glowering at Kevin and turned his gaze toward me. I smiled as best I could.

"We're trying to save the world, babe. Even if it means one zombie at a time, right?"

He held my gaze for a long moment and then shook my arm off. With a grunt, he started down the hall toward the bathrooms we'd seen the day before.

"I'm going to hit the showers," he muttered. "I don't suppose you left any fresh panties for me, eh Doc?"

He was gone before any of us could respond. My cheeks heated with blood at his comment and I looked at Kevin with an apologetic shake of my head.

"Sorry. He's a hothead," I muttered. "He'll come around."

Kevin smiled, but there was something kind of pity-ing about it. "I'm sure he has many wonderful qualities. And I'm sure he was a great help when you caught the zombie."

My brow wrinkled. "Well, to be fair, *we* caught the zombie."

But Kevin was already starting away from me and I didn't think he heard me as he turned the corner and left me standing in the sterile hallway with The Kid watching me, a little smug grin on his face.

By the time we had all showered (The Kid protested loudly, but we insisted. Two words for prepubescent boys: Pee. Ew.) at least a couple of hours had gone by. So when I stepped from the bathroom, my hair still damp and freshly dressed in a new t-shirt and cargo pants, I was surprised to see Dave waiting for me, arms folded, in the hall.

"Ready to load up?" he asked, his tone no longer the angry one from earlier.

I tilted my head. "What do you mean, load up?"

"I mean get the fuck out of here." He rested his head back against the wall with a heavy sigh. "Go to camp, get some rest. Get rid of The Kid and move on with our lives. Whatever."

I stared. "Dude, it's pitch black outside by now. There's no fucking way we're going out on the road now."

He pushed off the wall to face me. "Wait, are you suggest-ing we stay in Dr. Weird's Lab of Secrets for the night?"

I smiled, reaching for some kind of levity. "That sounds like a Harry Potter title."

He shook his head. "I'm not doing it, Sarah. I'm not staying here."

"Why?" I burst out in exasperation. "Because you don't like him? That's a stupid reason to go out to certain death and you know it."

When he didn't deny that, I moved closer and slipped my arms around his waist. With a smile, I leaned up to kiss him.

"Jealous Dave may be a Neanderthal, but he has to know he's the only boy for me."

Dave tried not to smile as he kept staring at the ceiling, but he failed. "Yeah," he said, "But Neanderthal Dave doesn't like his woman wearing other man's clothing."

I laughed. "Well, you can take them off... *if* you agree to stay here tonight like a good boy."

"Sarah is right."

Dave instantly tensed as Barnes's voice drifted from down the hall toward us. I sighed as the doctor approached us. So much for that hint of a good mood (and maybe even some nookie later).

"Thanks, I don't need your advice," Dave said as he let me go and glared at Barnes.

"You do if you're thinking of leaving. You can view the monitors yourself. Right now night vision shows twenty to thirty of those creatures at the warehouse entrance and I have no intention of wasting good ammo on them. Even if you got through, God knows how many hundreds stand between you and the camp."

Dave clenched his fists, but there was no arguing with that logic.

"Stay here tonight and I'll help you load up all your new materials for the fresh hunt tomorrow."

Dave snorted. "I don't think we've even established we're going on a new hunt for you tomorrow, Doc."

Barnes cocked his head. "Oh, I'm sorry. I understood from Sarah that you would be."

Dave turned toward me with a glare. "Did you now?"

"Dave—" I started, but he turned away.

"Well, she *is* the braaaains of our operation, right? Guess the brawn better get to bed and leave you two to plan our next step."

He took off down the hall toward—well, I don't really know where he was going, but he was pissed. Barnes's attempt to help had only made things worse.

But as I turned toward the doctor, I guess to apologize again, I caught the end of a smug smile on his face. It was gone almost instantly, but there was no denying its existence.

And that made me wonder what ulterior motive this guy had for causing problems. And how hard I'd have to work to solve them in the morning.

Dave put our fully loaded van into gear and drove away from the warehouse with morning sun glinting off the windshield cheerily. He hadn't spoken...not one fucking word...since we woke up.

I settled back in my seat and turned my head to look at him. I'd slept like a baby in the comfortable twin bed Kevin had provided, but Dave looked like hell. The circles under his eyes told me everything I needed to know without asking that good ol' sitcom conversation starter, "How did you sleep?"

"So you want to become dear Doctor *Kevin's* zombie hunter professionally now, eh?" he finally asked. "I thought you said we shouldn't confuse the 'brand.'"

I shut my eyes. With The Kid still in the back of the

van, I really didn't want to go into this, but apparently this was going to be the moment we hashed it out.

"Come on. You know all that brand stuff is bullshit now," I muttered.

He shot me a look. "You didn't think that before Barnes...I'm sorry, *Kevin* started asking you for favors. You were all about killing zombies for as much profit as we could manage."

"But that was when I thought all that was left was *this*," I said, waving my hands around at the empty desert. "In a wasteland, why not destroy, destroy, destroy? But now...I mean, come on, David. You saw what that serum did to the infected guinea pigs. You know that if Barnes could translate that to infected people it just might change everything. Don't you think that's nobler than just killing a bunch of zombies?"

He blew out a humorless laugh as he got off the freeway and made his way toward the camp. He had an answer on his tongue, but before he could say it, The Kid stuck his head between us and pulled his blindfold down away from his eyes. When he saw where we were, he gasped.

"Where the fuck do you think you're going?" he asked Dave.

I flinched. "Language!"

He ignored me, of course. Dave looked at him. "What? Where the fuck do you think we're going, Robbie? I'm taking you to the camp. You'll be safe there."

"No fucking way!" The Kid responded. "I'm not going to that camp."

I turned on him and the stress finally took over. "Look, you little brat, we're not taking you with us, so forget it.

In the camp you'll be taken care of. Why the hell wouldn't you want that?"

He folded his arms. "Have you ever seen the way they treat kids in the camp? Oh yeah, some of them, the little ones, get taken by some nice lady who lost her own brats. But most of them get put into one big fucking tent. Sometimes some religious jerk comes in and tries to teach us to pray or whatever. But we don't get to do shit. And we can't leave. It's prison. And I'm not going to fucking prison."

He touched the gun in his waistband and suddenly I felt a scene from *Boyz n the Hood* or something coming on. I rubbed my eyes with my fists hard enough to see stars. Seriously, the drama boys create...

"Well, what do you want us to do, Kid?" I finally asked as calmly as I could. "We can't just leave you running around in zombie hell. You may not like to hear it, but you're eleven years old. You're too young to make it on your own."

He shook his head and suddenly I saw just how determined he was in his eyes. "My mom died on the first day the zombies hit Phoenix. My dad... well, he's a whole other story. But the point is, I've been taking care of myself since the first moment this started. I didn't need a babysitter then. I don't now. So forget it."

Dave slammed on the brake and swerved to park at the side of the deserted road. He turned in his seat and stared at the scraggly little boy who had somehow taken over our van and apparently our lives.

"And what will you do if we just pull into the camp and drop you off? You know I could get that gun from you if I wanted to."

The Kid swallowed. Hard. He stared at Dave like he was sizing him up and by the pallor to his skin I'm guessing he knew he wouldn't win in a fight. There was a time when I wouldn't have thought Dave would ever take it that far, but now I wasn't so sure. He might not have been bluffing.

"Well, I guess I'd have no choice but to tell everyone what you're doing," The Kid said softly, and the hardness was back in his little boy eyes. "About catching zombies and cures and warehouses that hide labs somewhere, what...out past Sedona Street?"

I spun around in my own seat to look at him. The Kid had been wearing a blindfold both in and out of the warehouse, how the hell had he figured *that* out?"

He smiled like he was a mind reader. "I counted the turns," he explained even though I hadn't asked. "Point is, even if I just have a tiny clue of the location of your big, bad secret lab, somebody will figure it out. And then your doctor guy won't be so protected anymore."

"You little hustler," I breathed, though once again I was impressed by The Kid. Most people didn't figure out blackmail and extortion until they were in their teens, at least. But I guess zombie apocalypses make you grow up fast.

Dave sat for a long moment just looking at The Kid. Then he slowly faced forward again, let out a deep sigh, and put the van in gear. To my surprise, he swung it around on the wide road and turned away from the camp and back toward the Badlands.

"What the hell are you doing?" I asked.

He shrugged. "Unless you want to put your precious Kevin in danger, not to mention our own asses, I guess The Kid is right. He holds the cards."

I slid down deeper in my seat as I muttered to myself about jerk kids and birth control. But David was right, anyway. At this moment, we had no choice but to keep the brat with us.

"So," The Kid said with a grin wide enough to split his face. "What are we doing now? Catching or killing zombies?"

I sent a side glance toward Dave and he sent the same toward me. At the moment, nothing was really resolved and neither one of us was in a big damned hurry to flinch first in our fight.

Before one of us could, though, The Kid pointed. "Better decide fast. Look, a loner zombie!"

I followed where he was pointing. We had turned back onto the main road that led to the highway. The overpass was about a quarter of a mile away, a big wide hill that led east or west down the 202 depending on which way you turned.

At the top of that big hill was a pacing zombie, almost like he was waiting for something. He was exactly the kind we wanted to catch since he was alone and in an area where there wasn't much chance that something else was hiding. If we were going to keep catching, I guess a decision was going to have to be made about it.

Now.

We all stared as Dave slowed the vehicle to nothing more than a crawl. We were so far away that unless we made a big noise or did something else to draw attention to ourselves, a zombie wouldn't notice us.

Except that I could have sworn this one *did*. Its pacing slowed and it seemed to turn toward us and shift its weight.

"Get me the glock with the scope," I said softly, waving my hand in the back toward The Kid.

I heard him shuffling around and then felt the heavy weight of the semi-automatic in my palm. I lifted the gun and peered through scope.

The zombie was everything we'd come to expect from the living dead. Gray skin, black sludge caked around the mouth, rotting body. Only this one still managed to be different somehow. For one thing, he was bigger than your average zombie. I'm not talking *Resident Evil ridiculous*, of course, but this guy had been a big boy in life, bigger even than the Arnold Schwarzenegger wannabe zombie I'd lured to our net trap yesterday.

But that wasn't all that separated him from your average, run-of-the-mill infected bastard. Unlike the other zombies I'd seen over the past few months, his pacing had a purposeful quality to it. He wasn't just shambling aimlessly. He was waiting. Watching.

And in that moment, he lifted his head and he looked right at us. Through the high-powered scope I could see pretty good detail on his face. There was no doubt about it, he was really looking. *Seeing* us even though we were too far away for most zombies to notice through their rotting eyes.

He tilted his head back and let out a moaning groan that was loud enough to be heard even all the way at our car.

"Shit, David," I whispered, my tone laced with two emotions that bubbled inside of me like boiling oil. First there was fear, intense and powerful like I hadn't felt since that awful moment when we saw a zombie for the first time.

But there was something else, too. Excitement. My

heart raced with it and my hands shook as I continued to stare through the scope.

"What is it?" he whispered.

I lowered the scope and looked at him. "I think *that* might be a bionic zombie."

CHAPTER 10

Strive for the four-hour work week.
The rest of the time, run like hell.

Dave blinked as he looked at me. "What?"

I stared at him, overcome by the same disbelief that lined his face.

"*Bionic zombie*," I repeated on nothing but a trembling breath.

With a shake of his head, Dave snatched the gun from my hand. For a moment, he hesitated, almost as if he didn't *want* to look through the scope, but finally he lifted it and stared up the hill toward the pacing zombie.

I held my breath as I waited for him to say something, *anything*. But he didn't. He just stared and stared through the scope. For a long time the car was silent until he finally lowered the weapon.

"Shit," he muttered.

And that was all the reaction I got because just about the same time he finally said something the zombie started sprinting toward us. Sprinting. This wasn't a hunter jog or half-assed run. This was a Jackie Joyner-Kersee full-on *sprint* (minus the dragon lady nails, of course).

Now I don't know what came over us. I mean, we'd fought probably thousands of zombies by this point (just the steering wheel car count was in the hundreds) and we'd always won those battles, even if they were sometimes close. After all these months, though, we knew what to do. Hell, we got *paid* for what we do.

But I guess neither of us wanted any part of this shit until we had more time to figure it out.

"Reverse, reverse!" I screamed as Dave threw it into just that gear and floored it backward.

The poor Kid flew around the back of the veering van, crashing into the metal walls and grappling for any kind of purchase as Dave spun the wheel to turn away from the monster rapidly approaching our vehicle.

"Please stop doing that!" Robbie bellowed between grunts as he slid around the back.

We both ignored him. Right now getting away was more important. Plus, we had antibiotic cream and Sponge-Bob Band-Aids! He'd be fine.

Our tires screeched against the asphalt as Dave plowed forward, sending up a plume of smoke behind us that stank of burned rubber and dust. We tore off down the long, deserted road at sixty miles an hour.

Dave kept driving for fifteen minutes at full speed. He leaned over the steering column, silent and strained, his knuckles white around the wheel as he merely stared out at the road ahead of us.

In the back, The Kid had bundled up against one of the van walls, his knees pulled up to his chest. He was picking at one of his ratty shoes without looking at either of us.

Which left me. Shaking. Stunned. And wanting to talk about what I'd seen so bad that I just couldn't hold it in anymore. I finally turned toward David.

"It was bionic, wasn't it?" I whispered.

He jolted, almost like he'd forgotten the rest of us were in the vehicle with him. For the first time, he lifted his foot a little from the gas pedal and we slowed down to a more reasonable speed for the school zone we were currently streaking through.

Although, to be fair to Dave, the school had burned down weeks ago, the only kids left there were probably zombie monsters, and there were no cops to ticket him for going sixty-three in a twenty anyway.

"I don't know," he said. His voice was shaking a little and he drew a breath to steady it. "Maybe not. I mean, maybe it was just a coincidence that the ... *thing* was bigger and that it only *seemed* like it was ... um ... *aware* of us."

I stared at him. "Are you *that* jaded? That blind?"

He glared at me. "What do you mean?"

I expelled a breath of frustration. "I *mean* that people in the camps and on the street have been talking about bionics for a couple of days now, but you said you could only believe what you see."

"That's true, Sarah," Dave snapped. "It's crazy to chase rainbows just because someone told you there was a leprechaun with a fucking pile of Lucky Charms at the end."

I slammed my hands on the dash with enough force that it stung. "There *is* a motherfucking leprechaun, David! You just *saw* it. Just like you *saw* Kevin's cure in the lab a couple of days ago. And yet you still doubt both of those things. You're still looking for excuses as to why they aren't true. Why? Is it because you're scared?"

He slammed on the brake and in the back The Kid grunted pathetically as he slid on the metal van floor and sort of smooshed against the back of our seats.

Dave ignored his renewed whines and spun around to face me.

"Yes, I'm fucking scared, Sarah. And if you aren't then you're delusional and *crazy*. That *thing* back there, whatever it was, if it really is some kind of new breed of zombie that has even a fraction of higher brain function or greater strength...it means more of us are going to die."

"Not necessarily!" I said, but my tone had no strength to it.

"Yes, necessarily," he bellowed. "The only reason we have any chance against the horde now is that the zombies are stupider than Paris Fucking Hilton. They can't figure out tactics or find ways to work together on any real scale. So we have an advantage. If they start to think, even just a tiny bit, the advantage goes out the window."

I flinched, but he wasn't done. His voice elevated.

"And since we somehow convinced ourselves we have to make our living in this world by chasing things that go bump in the night, that means *we* might die. Or worse, get bitten so that one of us might have to kill the other before they go all undead on everyone's ass."

"So wait, are you saying no more zombie catching, even no more zombie killing?" I gasped.

He gripped the steering wheel with both hands until his knuckles turned white. "Neither one of those activities seems like it's going to ensure a nice old age with a retirement pension, Sarah."

I blinked as I stared down at my rough hands. Once upon a time, when I worked in an office job, they'd been soft. I'd even done home manicures and painted my nails all pretty. But today they were the hands of someone who worked to survive. Someone who had to.

But I missed manicures. I missed being able to sleep in on a Sunday and then have waffles. I missed being able to just watch bad television at night while I munched on microwave popcorn.

I missed normalcy even if I'd grown accustomed to not having it. Even if I'd accepted I'd probably never have it again.

I sighed. "I realize what you're saying," I said softly. "But I see what Kevin showed us in that lab. And I think *that* might help us get to an old age, though maybe not the pension."

"Christ Sarah—" he started.

I touched his face. "No, just listen to me. Really listen. What if Barnes is right? What if what he has really *is* a cure and all this could end? What if we could go back to the way things were? What if we *all* could?"

It was The Kid who answered, not David.

"No more camps," he whispered. Dave blinked before he looked back at him. The Kid was looking at us. "No more zombies to run from?"

I nodded, caught between my own hope and my desire not to give a child a false version of it.

"Maybe," I finally offered weakly.

"Do you think there's a Midwest Wall?" The Kid asked after a long hesitation.

I glanced at David. My husband didn't believe in any of that stuff. But he was sitting quietly, so I shrugged as an answer.

"I don't know. I've heard things, but we have to wait

out the winter up North before we even think about heading that way."

The Kid's shoulders slumped. "Oh." He was quiet for a long moment and then he surprised me by continuing, "See, I have this aunt who lives in Nashville."

"Yeah?" I encouraged him.

He nodded. "Maybe if there weren't zombies, she would come and get me."

I smiled. This was another one of those times when I remembered The Kid was, well, a kid.

"My mom lived in the middle of Illinois before the outbreak and I heard my Dad ran for Chicago when all this started," I said. "Maybe they'd come get me, too."

Dave smiled a little. "My parents are in Virginia," he said. "I guess they might want to get me if there weren't any zombies."

I laughed. "Are you kidding? You're probably on the back of milk cartons all over the East Coast. You're the beloved baby of that family."

His smile fell. We'd had to kill his sister when she turned zombie a few months back, so I guess that made him the only child now. I reached out and touched his arm as an apology for my stupidity.

"I'd rather say I tried to save the world than to wish I had," I said softly.

There was a long hesitation before Dave surprised me by nodding. "Okay, so I guess that means we keep catching for Dr. Doom in his underground lair."

I almost squealed in delight, but Dave looked so somber about the whole thing that I couldn't exactly feel happy about it.

"But that pulley thing isn't going to work on a regular

basis," he continued. "It's too limiting when it comes to hunting grounds and I don't like that it requires one of us to be up and away from the other."

"Hey!" The Kid said from the back.

Dave shot him a brief glance. "Other*s*. Sorry Robbie."

"So we need a new way to catch, I'm okay with that. Let's talk about it some more," I said, anxious to show him that I was totally down with working within his limits, as long as it meant I didn't have to quit.

"What about a net gun?"

Dave and I both froze before we slid around in our seats to look at the kid. He had a candy bar in his hand, though I swear I had no idea where it had come from, and he was looking at us like we were idiots.

"And just where are we going to get a net gun from?" I asked.

He shrugged. "Maybe Army Surplus, but you could make one, you know."

Dave blinked. "Really?"

He nodded with enthusiasm. "I read about it in the library."

I stared. "The library? Wait, you went to the library?"

Somehow I couldn't picture him curled up with a book like the kid from *The Neverending Story*. That seemed more Lisa Simpson than Bart.

He nodded like it was weird that I'd doubt him. "There's tons of stuff you can learn in the library, Sarah. You should try reading."

I bit my tongue and glared at Dave when he dared to laugh at the brat's little quip. "So do you remember what book the directions were in?"

Again The Kid nodded. "Sure, it was at the Desert

Sage branch of the library. You just need stuff from the hardware store."

Dave nodded and I started accessing the GPS to give us a route to the library that didn't include going back toward the bionic zombie. Although I could tell David wasn't happy about the prospect of doing this, his jaw was set as we took off.

I just had to hope that in the end, our decision to keep catching zombies for a man he apparently despised wouldn't be one he (or either of the rest of us) would regret.

Outside of the camps, the libraries were probably the most happening social scene in a post-zombie world. It was funny because before the outbreak, it was so hard to get people into them and so many had struggled with funding, but after...well, they provided entertainment, information, and comfort with their books and old magazines.

Unfortunately, the biggest local branch had been situated squarely in downtown Phoenix and had been totally destroyed in the firebombing. But lucky for us, the little Desert Sage location was far enough away from downtown and a low enough building that it hadn't suffered any damage from the government cleansing.

Eventually, survivors had boarded up the windows and reinforced the doors to keep the zombies from seeing the activity inside and coming to investigate. Instead of bright fluorescents that illuminated every corner, the lights were now only Coleman lamps and lanterns (we never risked candles with the books. See, we *could* have nice things now.).

Once inside, we milled around with about two dozen

other people. They were all kinds, from ones who were searching for information on building a shelter to building a nuclear device to kids curled up with *Huckleberry Finn* or *Anne of Green Gables*. Dave broke away from us and started hitting the others up for information about the new zombies and anything else of use.

Meanwhile, The Kid and I went to the back of the library, to a long-ignored corner where old-fashioned, hard-copy library catalog cabinets stood. When we opened them, they smelled like musty paper and ink, delightful. But I didn't have much time to enjoy the nostalgia. We had to find that book The Kid claimed had directions for a net gun.

And damn if the brat wasn't right. Not only was there a how-to book on that subject, but it contained all kinds of other useful build-it-yourself projects, too. If only the damned copy machine could be made to work....

I thought of Kevin's shining lab. I bet he had a copier I could use if we managed to bring back another zombie. I glanced around. There wasn't anyone nearby to see me, so I blocked the view of my backpack and gently opened it. The Kid stared at me as I gingerly slipped the book between all the other stuff inside my bag and then covered it up with the hoodie I had put on in the cool morning air.

Taking the books from the library had become a no-no since the outbreak. Especially books like this that could aid and assist other survivors in the fight.

What I was *really* supposed to do was place the book on the tables that had been shoved together in the center of the room. They were special books that contained everything a human in a zombie-crazed world could want. Books on water purification and agriculture and weaponry and building exactly the kind of shit you always saw on television on *Survivor* or *Lost* or whatever.

As I zipped back up, The Kid glared at me.

"So there are *no* rules anymore?" he asked.

I almost laughed. Now he was lecturing *me* on good and bad behavior? The same kid who had resorted to blackmail to get what he wanted just a few hours before?

I shook my head and glanced around to make sure no one had heard his annoyed statement. "Chill out. I'll bring it back after I see if Kevin can make a copy. He's got to have a copier in that lab."

The Kid shrugged. "Do you like him?"

I blinked. "Huh? *Who*, Kevin?"

The Kid nodded. "Yeah. I think he likes you."

Heat flooded my cheeks and I jerked my gaze across the library toward David. He was standing with some guy I didn't recognize having what looked to be a pretty intense conversation. Good thing, too. I doubted he'd like hearing what The Kid had to say.

"Don't be stupid," I hissed. "You don't have a girl you like, do you?"

The Kid made a face. "Ew. Girls? Um, cooties."

"Well, *that's* how I feel about Kevin. Dr. Barnes. And he doesn't like me, he just wants what I can give him."

I hesitated as I ran that sentence back in my head and realized it actually made the situation sound worse, not better. I hurried to correct myself.

"Zombies, I mean. He likes that I can bring him zombies for his lab."

The Kid looked incredulous, but then shrugged like he didn't care. "Whatever."

I jumped as Dave suddenly appeared beside us. "Whatever what?"

"Nothing," I said, a little sharper than I had intended to sound. Dave's brow wrinkled at my tone and he tilted his head like he was going to press further. I grasped for any subject to put him off the one The Kid and I had been discussing. "So any news from the others in here?"

It worked. Dave's concern and confusion fled, but his face grew long and worried over something else instead. "Not a lot, unfortunately. A few of them had more reports of . . . bionics or whatever you want to call them. No fights so far, at least none anyone has survived to report, but lots of distance sightings. It's starting to freak people out."

I flinched as I was forced to remember the zombie on the hill over the highway. I wanted to forget him, but he was on my mind constantly now.

Dave continued. "And that guy over there says no one has seen Jimmy No-Toes since the last time we got called out to see him."

I stared, my thoughts of super monsters fading a fraction. "*What? Really?*"

Dave nodded, grim. "Yeah. Apparently he was supposed to do some trading at the barbershop with some people. They waited half a day for him, but he never showed."

I shifted. "The guy is a flake, for sure, but that's not like him to avoid a trade meeting. If there's profit to be had, he wouldn't miss a date."

A sigh was Dave's response. "Don't get me wrong, the guy is a shit, but I don't like the idea of him getting zombiefied or anything."

The Kid shifted uncomfortably next to us and when

I looked down I was surprised to see how miserable he looked. Shit. It was so hard to remember he was just a boy in all of this. And sometimes talking about scary things made a child into a child again.

I motioned my head toward him and Dave blanched as he saw the same thing I did.

"Oh, Christ, Kid, I'm sorry," he said as he reached down to ruffle the boy's hair. "I'm talking out my ass. Probably this guy we're talking about just decided to take off for greener pastures."

All of us knew he was lying, but The Kid forced a smile anyway. Dave returned it and continued, "So, did you find your net gun instructions?"

The Kid looked at me. "Yeah. Sarah stole the book."

I shook my head. "Fucking tattletale."

Dave stared at me. "You're *stealing* the book?" he whispered after a brief glance around us.

I shrugged and decided not to mention my plans for favors from Kevin involving copy machines.

"I just thought it might help us not to have to copy everything by hand," I explained without looking at him.

Dave looked at me weird.

"I'll bring it back," I promised.

The Kid snorted, but we were blissfully interrupted when we were approached by some newcomers. I smiled as Josh and Drea, our friends from the camp, came into the library. They saw us and made a beeline in our direction.

"Hey, you two!" I said, relieved for their interruption. "Fancy meeting you here."

Drea hugged me briefly and waved at David, then she looked down at our companion.

"Who's your little friend?" she asked, though I caught

her sending a side glance at Josh. His normally friendly face was solemn and even sad as he stared at the little boy who stood with us.

The Kid glared at her. "I'm not little."

She shrugged. "Whatever you say."

"What's your name?" Josh asked quietly as he continued to stare at The Kid.

"Robbie," The Kid answered, but for once there wasn't anything snotty to his tone. He actually smiled at our friend briefly.

"He was helping me find a book," I offered as some kind of explanation as to why he was with us. I liked Josh and Drea a lot, but I wasn't ready to start spreading the word about what we were doing here.

"Well, I was looking for a book, myself," Josh said. "Want to help?"

The Kid shrugged one shoulder. "I guess."

The two of them started off toward the catalog where Robbie and I had looked up the book tucked into my backpack. Drea watched them go with a sigh.

"You okay?" I asked.

She nodded. "Yeah, I just hope *he* is."

"Why?" Dave asked as he looked off toward our friend and our unwanted guest. They were talking as they flipped through the cards together.

She blinked and I was surprised to see tears in her eyes. "Josh had a little boy. A bit younger than your kid, but..."

I flinched as her sentence trailed off. There was only one ending to it. "I had no idea."

"It's okay." Drea shrugged. "It just kind of hits him sometimes."

I nodded. We all had our moments.

Dave shifted in discomfort since there wasn't exactly anything you could say to make the situation better. "So what are you guys doing here?"

Drea stopped staring off into the distance and smiled as she swiped at her tears. "Doing a little research on chemical grenades. They might be good for distance fighting and clearing buildings that are already useless for anything else."

My eyes went wide at the idea. "Chemical grenades? Isn't that super dangerous?"

Drea nodded. "Yup."

Before we could press her further, Josh and The Kid came back with a card in hand.

"Pretty fucking dangerous," Josh interjected as he ruffled The Kid's hair. "But don't worry. I was *almost* Dr. Josh before the plague struck. I know what I'm doing."

"You're a chemist?" The Kid asked with wide eyes.

Josh nodded. "Or I would have been, anyway, if everything hadn't gotten all fucked up. But hey, I wanted to take a sabbatical anyway, so I guess this has been it."

Dave chuckled. "Huh, I like that. We've all just been on sabbatical."

"What's a sabbatical?" The Kid asked, his brow wrinkling.

"A vacation." Drea sighed as if the idea was heavenly. And it totally was.

The Kid shook his head as he started off toward the library entrance. "You guys are weird."

I couldn't help but laugh and so did the rest of them.

"I guess that's our cue to leave," Dave said as he saluted our friends briefly.

"Yeah." Josh looked after The Kid for a minute. "Take care of him."

"We will," I said softly.

"Bye!" The Kid said as he turned with a smile for our friends.

We said some brief good-byes to the pair and then followed The Kid. We found him waiting near the checkout desk, watching Josh and Drea head into the stacks.

"What's up with them?" he asked.

I shrugged. "Just good people, trying to make it out of a bad situation. Like the rest of us."

"If he's a chemist, maybe he could help us," The Kid said softly.

Dave shook his head. "Well, I don't know about that. There's no reason to tell our business to the world."

"At least not yet," I said as I steered our little group toward the doors that led to the library foyer. "But maybe in the future."

Dave nodded and as we exchanged a look I could tell we were on the same page. Nice since we hadn't been the past few days.

"Yeah, I could definitely see turning to them in the future," he said.

I shook my head. Right now the only future I could think about was the one that involved a new toy.

I grinned at the very thought. I'd always liked toys. "Let's get out of here and get to the hardware store. If we can get this gun built today, we could have a new zombie by tomorrow midday!"

Dave opened his mouth as if to say more, but then shut it again. I was almost glad. We'd been bickering way too much lately and I really didn't want to start round three with a library full of strangers and a child who was likely to blurt out that I had a secret boyfriend to my surprisingly jealous husband. Or a stolen book to what could quickly turn into a mob.

I led the way out of the building and into the desert sun. As soon as we were out the door, though, we were greeted by not only the late morning heat and the sparkling blue sky, but a collection of three zombies pacing around our van across the small parking lot.

The area around the library was known to be a "no shooting" zone. It wasn't mandatory or anything, I mean there weren't exactly cops or anyone to police that, but it was a matter of common sense.

Shooting a zombie was the easiest and fastest way to kill it, of course, but it was also the loudest. Shooting often brought *more* of the living dead flooding to an area, looking for the source of the big noise. And since the library was a hub for humans, we really didn't want to create a fast-food joint for the shambling horde by alerting them to our presence here. Would you like fries with that brain? Supersize it?

"Machetes and clubs, please," I whispered as we edged closer to our van.

I pulled out the cool bat with the blade Dave had created for me. He went for his machete and even The Kid pulled what looked like a police baton from one of the many loops on his cargo pants.

"Ready?" Dave asked.

I nodded and then squared up my body in preparation for battle.

"Hey!" I called out to get their attention...or whatever you want to call it. "Dumb asses."

The zombies stopped pawing at the van door and slowly turned to face us. After so many months, all the undead were in an advanced stage of rot, though they seemed to hit that stage and then just...*stay* there. I don't know how the chemical interaction worked, but I guess it was something like zombie botox. You know: *keep eating brains, never age a day past disgusting*.

Their clothing, though, didn't get the benefit of daily brains injections. Or washing. So while at the beginning of the outbreak, you saw zombies in suits, uniforms, and bathrobes and could easily identify what they were doing before all hell broke loose, now it was harder. Cotton clothing was the first to fray away. Anyone who got turned wearing 100 percent cotton was now roaming around like Adam and Eve. Trust me, there is nothing more disturbing than rotting jiggly parts. Blech!

But other fabrics held up better. For instance, the group in front of us contained a nurse. Her polyester uniform had kept up pretty well, though it had long since stopped being pristine white. Red, sludgy black, and filthy brown were now her United Colors of Benetton. Her shoes had fared worse, though. She was missing one and the other was filled with holes and I swear I saw a cockroach climb from one to the other before she started moving.

She was joined by two male zombies. One was a cotton wearer so he was butt-ass naked except for what had once apparently been the waistband of a pair of jeans. The pockets were still attached to it and flopped around in the breeze along with his...er...bits and pieces.

The third zombie was a smaller girl. Maybe in her late teens, and her demin skirt was clean and fresh enough that

I had to guess she'd been turned sometime in the last few weeks, rather than earlier in the outbreak.

I would have felt a bit sorry for the girl except that at that moment the three zombies started for us with growling grunts and a lot of angry tooth gnashing.

"I'll take Nurse Betty," I said as I started toward the zombies. "You take Bits and Pieces."

"I've got Miley Cyrus," The Kid said and forward we charged.

As the zombies swarmed, I turned my attention on the nurse. Her fingers clawed, with long, chipped pink fingernails grown out and slashing the air around me.

I dodged her attempts to grab me and swung my bat. I connected with her neck rather than her head and there was a crack. Her neck twisted at an awful angle, but she only grunted with frustration before she grabbed my arm in a literal death grip and started to yank me forward. I jammed the knife blade at the end of my bat toward her and slashed her face.

Again, she only winced a little, but continued to shake me like a rag doll as she moved me toward her ever-biting mouth.

But the third time was the charm and this time when I stabbed at her, my blade pierced her forehead and slid into her brainpan with the ease you'd expect from cutting a boneless chicken breast.

The infected woman howled this time and thrashed, but that only made the blade scramble around in her skull and quickened the inevitable. With a whine, she slumped and my bat yanked free, the sharp blade severing the top of her head as she fell at my feet.

I turned to offer assistance to The Kid first, but found

that he was already done and wiping the blunt baton off on what had once been the younger zombie's jean skirt. He looked bored by it all and gave me a look.

I turned to Dave, but he too was finished. His machete dripped as he sliced it through the air around the headless, naked body of the male zombie. Apparently I had been the only one to have a bit of trouble with my zombie. Maybe it was all the distraction of late, but I didn't like that I'd been a bit weaker than the rest, including a fucking *child*.

"Well, now that *that* little chore is done," I said in a falsely bright tone, "how about we hit the Lowe's up the street?"

Dave was watching me. Maybe he'd noticed my uncharacteristic struggle with my zombie, but he didn't say anything. He just unlocked the van and got into the driver's seat to drive us to our net-gun-making future.

CHAPTER 11

Think win-win. You probably won't get it,
but think it.

Although we had directions and all the PVC piping and netting materials we could ever want, need, or *hate* at the Lowe's down the street from the library, creating the gun wasn't as easy as the directions implied. In fact, it took us all the way until dark to get the damn thing even half made. There were at least three tantrums during the exercise (and only one of them was The Kid having a meltdown) and one half-assed threat of divorce (from David to me when I got tired and cried...just a little).

But by the time the morning light started peeking back through the broken glass doors of the home improvement store, we were looking at a net gun.

It was jacked up. It was ugly as hell. I think some parts of it were held together with only duct tape and a prayer, but it was a net gun. And as our five test runs with it had proven, it would work. In fact, we had caught a barbeque, several lawn chairs and even a pallet full of useless grass seed with it.

Surely those were viable replacements for writhing, biting, highly infected zombies who were just itching to devour our brains, right?

I guess we were tired, because at that point, we thought so. I smiled at Dave as he carefully reset the netting into the contraption. It had to be done perfectly or the gun wouldn't fire.

"Think it will work?" I asked.

He shrugged even as he stifled a yawn. "I like it better than the stupid pulley system. At least we don't have to be right on top of a zombie to get him netted."

I nodded with enthusiasm. "So let's get out there!"

He stared at me in blank disbelief. "We've been up all night fucking around with this, Sarah."

"I know," I said with a laugh. "But I have a new toy now and I want to play with it."

He didn't laugh with me. In fact, his dour mood was starting to bum me out. "Do you *really* want to go out and get into a fight with zombies while we're exhausted? Especially after what happened yesterday?"

I flinched and turned my full focus on him. He was frowning at me, his face lined with worry and upset.

"And just what do you mean by *that*?" I asked though it was completely obvious to what he was referring.

"Yesterday you could hardly put down one zombie," Dave said softly. "And we both know full well that catching is way harder and far more dangerous than killing."

I stared at him. Not since the beginning of the outbreak had he actually questioned my abilities. He had been protective over the last few months, but never judgmental. So this was a new thing and I didn't like it. Not one fucking bit.

"You know, *everyone* has an off day," I ground out past clenched teeth. "And *you* were just barely flicking the blood off your blade when I was done. So that means it took me what, one *minute* longer to take care of Nurse Betty than it did for you to take care of Ugly Naked Zombie?"

He held my gaze evenly. There was no hint of apology in his stare as he said, "A minute is an eternity, Sarah. A minute can mean the difference between safety and me having to put you down before you turn into a monster."

I opened my mouth to argue, but he plowed on without letting me. "You know that as well as I do. We've both seen the same fucked-up crap over the past few months."

"That's bullshit," I snapped, even though I knew it wasn't. "You are just so against anything to do with this mission that you are willing to say and maybe even *do* anything to sabotage it."

"If anything is bullshit about this situation, *that* is. Come on—" he started, but I wasn't about to hear it.

I snatched the net gun from his hands. "*I'm* going out to try out our new weapon and catch me a zombie. You're welcome to come with me or not. Whatever."

I turned on my heel and started for the door, but I admit I was listening for him behind me, hoping he'd say exactly what he said next.

"Come on, Robbie," he called out, frustration still lacing his strained voice.

The Kid had gotten into one of those fake beds they have in home and department stores to show off their comforters and burrowed down in the covers with a comic book he'd gotten from one of his many pockets. I swear, he was like a secret agent with all that shit. Double-O-Annoying at your service. License to pester.

"We're going," Dave continued to call back into the unseen depths of the store. "If you want to stick with us, it's time to mount up."

I heard a lot of grumbling as I pushed my way through the once-automatic doors, but when Dave came out a couple minutes later, The Kid was trailing at his heels, rubbing his bleary eyes and muttering to himself about crazy grown-ups and stupid ideas.

I smiled with relief as I got into the driver's side of the van and started her up, setting the net gun awkwardly between the two front seats so one of us could have easy access.

The drive was uncomfortably quiet. Robbie was still half-asleep and jostled around gently in the empty expanse of the back of the van. For once, I wished he would talk so that I wouldn't have to face the fact that Dave and I were still pissed.

Still when I looked at my husband from the corner of my eye, he was scanning the area for zombies. Even angry, he was dependable and I appreciated that.

Especially when he held up a hand to catch my attention and said, "Two o'clock."

I followed his direction and saw two zombies about three hundred yards away down the long, wide road we had been following through town. They were hunched over a wrecked car that had flipped onto its side, its passenger windows facing the sky and wheels occasionally turning when the car was jostled to one side or another.

It was a late model sedan of no real description. It looked like every other car on the road had before the outbreak. Just the run-of-the-mill family car that got taken to church and the store and to soccer practice by a distracted mom or a weekend dad.

I know that's probably disappointing to all you Mad Max, post-apocalyptic junkies who figure the second the shit hits the fan, we're all going to start modifying our vehicles with flame throwers, but it just doesn't happen. Or at least, not this early in the game. The *Road Warrior* types tended to get eaten because they were stupid and took silly risks at the front end of the outbreak.

So this wasn't a *Road Warrior* Special, but just a car. From how little rust marred the dark paint, it appeared it had been driven until recently and even taken care of on some level. At least until it clipped the front end of an older wreck that was sticking half out in the road. In one instant, with one mistake, that older wreck had flipped this car onto its side the way it was now.

The accident had to have been recent, not only because of the lack of desert wear on the car, but because the two zombies actually had an interest in it.

See, the infected, they didn't seem to have any desire to eat older dead bodies. They wanted live victims or ones that had just bitten the dust less than five or six hours before. There was something about fresh meat, fresh brains that gave them what they wanted. And right now they were shaking and quaking, almost with excitement, though the living dead don't actually seem to feel any real emotion, as they reached in and out of the car with bloody fingers.

"Get the net gun ready," I said softly as I slowed the car to a crawl and inched toward the pair of them. "And Robbie, wake up. We may need your help if we have uninfected victims in the car."

The little boy suddenly popped his head between us and stared off toward the zombies.

"You think there might be people still alive in there?" he asked with a shiver.

I nodded. "With all that interest, I'd guess it's a strong possibility."

His head disappeared, but I heard him moving around in the back and loading up weapons. As we came to a stop about a hundred yards from the flipped car, he leaned forward and handed me a rifle and a 9mm, both fully loaded. I looked back toward him in surprise.

"Thanks, Kid. You might come in handy after all."

He grinned and I swear he also blushed, but Dave interrupted our "moment" by maneuvering the net gun into his lap.

"Talk later. Let's do this," he muttered through clenched teeth.

I nodded. "I'm going to roll up until I'm as close as I can get. Take the shot and get one of them if you can. One of us will shoot the other and then we can deal with whatever's in that car."

Dave nodded and slowly rolled the passenger window down fully. After some grunting, he managed to get the unwieldy net gun positioned to point it outside. He had his hand on the release mechanism when I started to roll forward again, doing my best to be both silent and deadly.

The zombies were so focused on whatever they were eating that they didn't even notice. Perfect.

"Now!" I whispered just beneath my breath.

Dave shot me a glare (apparently he didn't need my direction) before he lined up the gun as best he could and released the net toward the male zombie who was leaning over the car. The thing looked almost nonchalant, like a mechanic looking at your car to say, "Well, *there's* your problem, lady. Your car's been swarmed by zombies."

All the zombie needed was a cigarette hanging from his mouth and it would have been beyond perfect. Until the net hit him.

Pallets and lawn furniture didn't do justice to what it was like to catch a zombie in a glorified butterfly net. He flew back against the car as the net closed around him, pinning him to the metal.

His feet went out from under him and he collapsed back, thrashing and whining as he clawed and chewed helplessly at the netting. His movements only tangled him more, though, and unlike a human who would probably stop thrashing once the contraption started to twist and hurt him, the zombie didn't. Soon he was all wrapped up, mangled arms bent at odd angles behind and above him, and legs all akimbo.

Meanwhile the other zombie who had been half in the car window, pawing at whatever was left in there, popped out, his face covered with blood and his red eyes bright with killing frenzy. He turned toward us with a guttural, angry roar.

"Gun!" Dave hollered.

The Kid handed forward a semi-automatic M1A and Dave repositioned himself on the window ledge. He fired off a shot just as the zombie lunged toward him and the creature dropped straight down and out of our line of sight with just a final whimper.

"Go, go!" Dave said as he immediately launched out of the van and hustled toward the flipped car with me and Robbie right behind him.

I thought he might go for the captured zombie first,

since I had no idea how long he would stay stuck by the netting, but instead Dave went to the window of the vehicle without even double-checking our quarry (talk about making mistakes that could get a person killed, *David*).

He yanked away from the vehicle almost immediately and when he looked at me, his face was pale.

"What?" I whispered, nudging The Kid to keep his guns trained on the zombie as I moved to the window myself.

I peeked inside. It was a bloody mess but what had happened was clear enough. A girl probably about Robbie's age was in the back, her head caved in from the impact of the accident. But by the blood around her mouth and on her nails, it seemed like maybe she had been turned *before* the car flipped. She had obviously attacked the younger boy who was next to her on the seat, slumped against the door. He was what the zombies had been eating and it wasn't a pretty sight.

Dad had been driving and was apparently distracted by the kids "fighting" in the backseat (I wondered if he'd told them he was turning the car around if they didn't stop. My dad had always said that and it never worked, either). Their battle royale had probably led to the accident that ironically ended the girl's killing spree and was why poor old Dad was now half sticking out the windshield, killed by the accident before the zombies went for him.

I guess he should have buckled up for safety like those old public service announcements used to sing.

"Shit," I muttered as my stomach unexpectedly turned.

See, after three months of apocalypse, this kind of thing was actually rarer than it had been at the beginning. We used to see this all the time and had gotten numb to the violence and heartache of it in some ways.

But after at least a month of only finding victims who had died during a fight they'd chosen to take…well, a scene like this, a scene of a family turned upside down and ultimately destroyed by the infection…it was disturbing all over again.

"I've got to shoot," Dave said softly, his lips thinned with grim determination. "I'd guess they could wake up any time."

I nodded. There were varying amounts of time it took for a person to reanimate or change after a zombie attack. It was all based on where they were bitten and if they were killed by the attack or just injured. We pretty much knew the timetable by heart, but since we hadn't seen the accident, there was no way to be certain how much time was left before we would be involved in a father-son game called *Kill the Humans*.

It's almost like a three-legged race, but with more blood and screaming.

"Want me to do it?" I asked.

"No," he snapped as he motioned me away. "Go take care of your precious zombie."

I hesitated, but Dave put his back toward me as he leveled his gun on the child in the back seat. As I turned away, the car rocked from the first explosion of gunpowder.

The Kid and I both flinched as I moved toward him. The caught zombie was still snapping at Robbie, his fingers pushed through the spaces in the net so that they twitched and closed around air.

"Nice specimen," I said with false brightness. "It should be worth a couple of showers and maybe some new shoes and some food, eh?"

The Kid glared at me. "How about something useful like grenades?"

I laughed. "Okay, we'll ask. Though I'm not sure I like the idea of you running around with the ultimate fireworks."

The Kid's eyes lit up like he hadn't thought of that before but then he sobered at just about the same time that Dave fired his second shot behind us.

"Without the thing hanging in the air, it's going to get tougher to bind it up," The Kid said softly, watching around me for Dave as he came over to us.

Dave's face was pale and grim, but he managed a smile and a nod for the boy. "Yeah, but we'll figure it out. Go get the rope, huh?"

As The Kid scurried off to get rope and a burlap sack for our "guest," I returned my attention to David. "You okay?"

He shrugged. "We haven't had to shoot a victim in a long time," he said quietly. "It just reminded me of Amanda. And Gina."

I frowned. Amanda had been our neighbor who Dave had been forced to shoot in our car during our initial escape from Seattle. And Gina was his sister. When she turned, *I* had been the one to take care of her (and Dave afterward), but the particulars didn't matter. Even all these months and all these kills later, Dave was still haunted. I guess all of us survivors were, we just covered it up most of the time. But there were moments...there were always moments.

I touched his shoulder as The Kid came running back up with the rope. "There are no more sacks, sorry."

Dave swore under his breath as he grabbed the rope. "Shit. See, we should have taken our time better this morning. We could have cleaned out some supplies from the hardware store, but we weren't paying close enough attention."

I winced since the comment was directed toward me, but bit my tongue. "Maybe we can figure something else out for his head. Let's just tie him up for now."

Dave said nothing, just unraveled the coil of rope as he stared at the thrashing, hissing zombie. He was becoming increasingly loud as he looked from one of us to the other, trying to figure out if he could reach us and which one he wanted to eat first.

Finally, Dave shouted, "Will you please *shut up*!"

He was only venting, but to my surprise, it worked. The zombie's jaws snapped shut and he stared at Dave almost like he understood him. But then the moment faded and he immediately started back into wails and groans of anger and distress.

"Fuck me, it's worse than a damn cat in heat," Dave muttered. He motioned to me impatiently. "Now come help me."

I moved to his side. "So what, grab sides of the net and then try to hold him still while Robbie ties him up?"

Robbie took the rope from Dave and nodded. We exchanged a quick look and then each of us took a side of the twisted net. In one swift motion we flipped the zombie over so that he was face down and less likely to get to us with his gnashing teeth. We wrapped the net tightly around his back, holding him still as best we could.

Robbie jumped in between us, his small hands working swiftly as he tied a loop around the creature. Once his arms were bound tight at his sides, we started to roll him, wrapping him in the rope the same way we had with the other zombie a couple of days before.

The creature howled out his frustration with every spin, biting at us every time he faced us. But he was pretty much impotent by that point. Without him being able to scratch or grab us, his teeth were easy to avoid. The flying sludge from his mouth sprayed against our arms, but his teeth didn't find a home in our flesh.

I sighed as we finally let him go and he hit the ground with a thud, his face down in the dust so that his grunts were mercifully muted.

"What about his head?" I asked.

The Kid had to sit in the back of the van with the *thing* that now sputtered in the dirt before us and I didn't want him to have to dodge teeth the way he'd have to if we didn't get the zombie's face covered.

"What about a t-shirt?" The Kid asked, tugging his dirty one off his head to reveal his little chicken-y arms and chest.

"Great!" Dave said with a smile for him.

We flipped the zombie again and pulled him to a seated position. His garbled sounds of anger were muffled as we wrapped his head in the dirty white cotton t-shirt. I hoped he didn't still have a sense of smell because p-u! That child had some body odor. A normal human would not have been able to survive, that's for sure.

Finally we got our unhappy guest into the back of the van with The Kid sitting watch over him. And when I say over him, I mean it literally. The zombie was face down and The Kid sat on the middle of his back, holding him still as we took off.

Midday sun filtered down on us as we got back on the highway and headed back toward Kevin's lab. With the temperature rising in the van, the smell of rotting flesh had both Dave and I rolling down our windows. As I drove, I wished I could put my head outside like a dog and just let the breeze fill my nostrils instead of the rancid smell of rotting, dead flesh inside.

"Put Febreze on the shopping list," I choked as I got off on the now familiar exit and turned toward the lab.

Dave smiled, but that was as good as it got. I frowned as we came up over the hill and started the last half mile or so to the warehouse and the release of our stinky companion to Dr. Barnes. I could see the sunlight glinting off the slumped metal roof of the place, we were almost there...

And that's when the zombie got his arm free.

CHAPTER 12

Protect your brand...and your ass.

Even though the zombie mind was broken and infected by God knew what, even though they had no drive other than to kill and devour people...you had to give them credit. When it came to that drive, they were awesomely good at what they did. They had no fear, so they were willing to hurt themselves, to throw themselves off a cliff if it meant reaching a victim and feeding their never-ceasing desire for brains and flesh.

And that's what this one did (or so we figured out later). He had dislocated his own shoulder in order to get free of the binds around him. The arm came up in my rearview mirror and before I even had the chance to scream or warn anyone else in the van, he had The Kid by the throat.

"Fuck! It's free!" I shouted, glancing over my shoulder. We swerved and I forced myself to pay attention to the road, straightening out the wheel, but not before we started to skid on the loose gravel along the shoulder.

Dave unbuckled and flung himself into the back of the vehicle in one smooth motion.

"Fuck, fuck, fuck!" he cried.

In the rearview mirror, I could see the three of them sliding around on the metal cargo area of the van. Somehow the zombie had gotten his other arm out of his binds, which basically made him completely free. A few ropes around his waist and a child-sized t-shirt at his neck weren't going to stop him, that was for damn sure.

With a growl, the zombie flipped over on top of The Kid before Dave could get a good grip on him. Robbie screamed and flopped in a desperate attempt to get free, but the creature was immovable. It leaned down, pressing its rotting, black teeth against the soft cotton of Robbie's t-shirt in an attempt to gnaw on the child beneath him.

Dave flung his arms around the zombie and pulled back as hard as he could and the two fell across the side wall of the van at a weird, twisted angle.

Of course, I had to watch all this unfold in the rearview mirror, while at the same time I fought to control the vehicle. And it w*as* a fight, because the van was completely out of control thanks to the shale on the shoulder. My brake was to the floor, but we kept sliding at an awful sideways angle. It took every ounce of strength in my arms to keep the vehicle from going completely off the street.

I failed.

The shoulder suddenly turned to a full-on embankment and that was it. We skidded a few more feet and then we were rocking, off-balance. We flipped and for a slow-motion moment I thought of the other car. The one where we'd found our current zombie companion.

How long would it take for the infected to flood *our*

vehicle? To pull pieces of our bodies out and eat them while we still moaned in horror at the sight of it?

I hoped I'd die first so I wouldn't have to see.

Then my thoughts were gone. The van rolled onto its roof. I heard The Kid and David grunting and the zombie moaning as they flew all around the back of the van. Their bodies banged against the neatly organized weapons cache that lined the walls and thudded against each other as they fought to avoid the still-clawing zombie fingers.

As for me, I was still buckled in (unlike Dear Old Dad in the earlier wreck) so I stayed in my seat, my body fighting against the strap with a painful series of tugs and thrashes.

The van was still sliding on its roof, but it was slowing down as it glided through sand and dust and the thin roots of desert plants. But the slide stopped abruptly when we hit something on my side of the car. Momentum made my head snap to the side and collide with the edge of my partly rolled-down window.

Stars erupted in front of my eyes as the world moved into a strange, surreal half-time movement. It was almost like I'd slipped into some kind of weird movie. I felt movement, I heard sounds. One of them was someone saying my name, slow and steady, "Saaarrraaaahhh..."

And then there was nothing else.

There was a bright light in my eyes. Like the kind a doctor or a dentist shines in your face at their office. Had I had a surgery? If so, there were some fucked-up dreams I'd been having.

"Sarah?" a voice said from what felt like was very far away. "Sarah, it's time to wake up."

I recognized the voice, but it wasn't a family member. I had the odd, disconnected feeling that it *was* a doctor's voice. Only there was something else that fluttered on the edge of my foggy memory. Something bad.

"David?" I squinted into the light, trying to make out the unseen person behind it.

There was a slight hesitation that made my heart leap, but then the person said, "He's fine. Neither he nor the boy were badly hurt in the accident. They're just putting the zombie in one of the lab rooms."

I squeezed my eyes shut as clarity began to seep back into my cloudy mind. The boy. The *zombie*. Suddenly tears stung my eyes and I lifted a hand to cover my face.

"Shit," I muttered as I swiped at the wetness that now covered my cheeks. "For a minute, I thought it was all a nightmare."

The light that had been shining in my face was pushed away and when I moved my hand I saw that the soothing voice I'd heard was indeed a doctor, but it was Dr. Barnes. Kevin was pale and concerned as he leaned over me.

"I'm sorry," he said softly. "I wish I could say it was. But no."

"You said accident?" I said as I struggled to sit up.

A blast of intense pain rocketed its way through my head like I'd put a shotgun to my temple and pulled the trigger, but somehow managed to survive the experience. I sucked in a breath as nausea overwhelmed me and forced me to cling tight to the edge of the bed as I rode out the feeling.

When my mind had cleared a small fraction, I looked around in an attempt to get my bearings. I was in one of the lab rooms just like the one we'd put the first zombie in a few days before. There were even straps along the side of my bed, though I wasn't in them, thank goodness.

"You don't remember the accident?" Kevin asked as he leaned over me to look at my face. I shook my head and he smiled, giving me that "cute-geek" feeling again. "Don't worry. You have a mild concussion."

I glared at him. "This is fucking *mild*?"

He gave me that same compassionate yet blank stare all doctors seem to have in their repertoire. The one that says, *I care, but I'm going to forget you in five minutes*.

"Actually, yes," he reassured me. "And a little memory loss is actually very common with the kind of head injury you suffered when the van flipped. The details will likely come back to you over the next few days."

"Well, can you fill me in a little sooner?" I asked as I collapsed back on the pillows behind me.

"Of course. You skidded on the shoulder of the road just outside my building. That gravel can be a killer, especially at high speeds. You lost control and ultimately hit an old telephone pole." He shook his head. "Thank *God* I was watching for your return and saw what happened in the monitors. I was able to get out to you right away."

"Sarah?"

I leaned around the doctor to see David at the door. The entire right side of his face was one big bruise and there was blood seeping from a small cut at the start of his hairline.

"Oh my God," I burst out as he came into the room and grabbed me for a painfully hard hug. When he finally let me go I reached up to brush at his bruise gently. "I'm sorry, I'm so sorry."

"Why?" he asked in a shocked tone.

I shook my head. "I was driving, I should have been more careful. I don't remember—"

Dave pulled back. "The zombie we got for Dr. Nobody here got free, Sarah. *That's* why you lost control. It had nothing to do with you being careful or not."

"What?" I asked, my foggy brain searching for memory of what had happened. I vaguely recalled a rotting arm lifting up in my rearview mirror and shut my eyes with a shiver at the thought.

"But you're okay?" I asked, my voice shaking. "And The Kid wasn't hurt?"

Dave frowned. "He sprained his wrist pretty bad, but I splinted it and he's managing. And his leg is all banged to hell."

"Oh no!" I burst out.

Hey, The Kid was a twerp, but I didn't want to hurt him… well, at least not this way. Strangle him like Homer Simpson might was more my fantasy.

"No, no," Dave insisted. "He's okay. He went to take that shower you kept ragging him about. The zombie got a lot of sludge on him when he attacked Robbie."

I winced. Yes, I vaguely recalled that, too, now that Dave mentioned it. The entire situation could have been so much worse. I could hardly breathe when I pictured all the ways it could have gone even more wrong than it had.

"She's okay?" Dave said, this time speaking to Kevin.

The doctor cleared his throat. "It's a minor concussion. The small cuts on her face will heal on their own, I stitched the larger one. Otherwise, she's okay."

I lifted my hand to my face and felt swollen cuts across my left cheek and a painful line of stitches near my ear on the same side. There was a mirror near the bed and I grabbed it to see. I groaned.

I was pretty much a mess and not even a hot one. My face was puffy, bruised, and scattered with scratches that I guess must have happened when I banged my face on the window. I vaguely recalled a crash of glass at some point during the accident.

"Now, do you want to tell her what *you* did when you found us?" Dave asked.

I put the mirror down and looked at the two men. Dave was still standing next to me, not looking at Kevin, but his entire body was laced with undeniable tension and fury. As for the good doctor, he had backed up and was standing behind my husband. In that moment, he looked like he wanted to bludgeon him with whatever was at hand. Currently it was just a clipboard, which was sort of a funny idea.

"What's going on?" I asked softly when a full two minutes had passed without a word from either one of them. "Did something happen after the accident that I need to know about?"

"When I approached the vehicle, I checked on you—" Kevin started.

Dave spun around, fists clenched at his sides and eyes wild with anger. "*After* that, asshole! What the fuck did you do after that?"

Kevin hesitated, but his gaze never left David's. "Seeing that the zombie was almost entirely free from his binds and that he was threatening both the child and David, who were pinned by the wreckage, I injected him with a serum."

"A serum?" I repeated, watching the two men in

confusion. My brain was still foggy and I didn't really get what was going on.

"He knocked the fucker out with some kind of drug, Sarah," Dave snapped.

I drew back with a shake of my intensely painful head that I immediately regretted. As I sucked in a breath and touched my skull, I said, "N-No, that's not possible. We've tried all kinds of sedatives since the outbreak, from Luminal to horse tranqs to fucking heroin. They just don't work on the dead."

"Well, *this* one did." Dave's voice was dangerously soft and almost gentle, but his expression was anything but. He looked ready to kill. "The zombie went down like he'd been shot."

"How do you know he wasn't dead?" I asked. "Maybe he took a blow to the skull in the wreck that put him down."

Dave arched a brow. "He isn't dead. His hands kept moving, his lungs kept filling even though the dead asshat doesn't need to breathe to live. He was still living dead, Sarah. Just down for the count."

"How?" I breathed in utter disbelief as I stared at Kevin again. "How is that possible?"

The doctor sighed slightly. "You're correct when you say it isn't possible. At least not traditionally. Normally the infected system doesn't allow for distribution of a sedative. The blood no longer flows since the host is dead, rendering drugs of any kind ineffective."

"Then how did what you did work, *Doc*?" Dave insisted.

Kevin glared at him. "I admit, I've done some testing using the head specimens in my lab. I developed a sedative that uses the zombie virus itself to drive forward to the brain of the infected."

I stared. "You use the zombie virus *on* zombies?"

He nodded. "It's a remarkable agent—"

Dave interrupted him with a snort. "You *would* think so."

Kevin ignored him, though his jaw tightened. "—it's almost totally self-driven. It doesn't require a beating heart to make its way to the brain."

I blinked. "Th-That's remarkable," I said with a smile over Dave's head at him.

He smiled back. "Thank you."

Dave was less impressed. "Before you start sucking his dick over this wonderful invention, I have a question, *Doc*. How long have you had this miracle *serum* in your possession?"

I stared at Kevin. To my surprise he was going pale, his eyes wide and filled with something like guilt merged with intense and righteous anger.

"Well?" I asked, my voice as soft as Dave's, though less accusatory.

"I came up with the formula about a month ago."

"He had this *miracle* the entire time we've met with him and he never thought to offer it to us, even though we're out there with our asses hanging out trying to snag him some monsters," Dave snapped, turning on me like I needed convincing. "We could have avoided the whole accident today if we'd just had some of that shit on us."

Dave was right, of course. But I clung to the hope that maybe it wasn't some kind of nefarious thing that had kept the doctor from sharing his invention with us.

"Why *didn't* you give it to us, Kevin?" I asked, trying

to ignore my throbbing head and sore body to concentrate on the very important answer.

He shrugged. "I hadn't been able to test it on a true live specimen, just like the cure for the infection," he explained with a sheepish shift. "I wasn't certain it would work until the moment I injected your specimen out in the van. I certainly had no idea how long the drug would be effective or what was the proper dose."

I looked at Dave. He was leaning on a piece of equipment in the room, just staring at the doctor. And although Barnes's explanation made logical sense to me, Dave remained angry.

"Can you give us a minute?" I asked as I reached out to take David's hand.

Kevin hesitated and then nodded as he backed out of the room and closed the door behind him. Once he was gone, I looked at my husband evenly.

"You okay?"

He shook off his angry glare to look at me with worry. "*Me? You're* the one who lost consciousness." He squeezed my fingers gently. "It scared the shit out of me, Sarah."

I nodded. "Sorry, I'll try not to do it again."

When he smiled slightly, I continued, "You know, you can't be so hard on the guy. I can understand not wanting to give us something that might not work and having us get hurt when we depended on it."

Dave stared at me for a long moment before he shook my hand off and backed away a step. "Gotta defend him, eh Sarah?"

"No!" I held up my hands in a gesture of surrender mostly because I was too fucking tired and hurt to argue about this. "I mean, he *could* have told us and offered us the opportunity to try the stuff out in the field. He *should* have. But come on. The guy was a lab rat before the outbreak, and now he hasn't had human interaction for months. He isn't so great at it if you haven't noticed."

Dave shrugged. "He seems to do just fine when it comes to *interacting* with you."

I stared in total disbelief. "Is all this piss and vinegar because you're *jealous* of Barnes? Are we on the fucking *Bachelor* now?"

He didn't answer for a long time, long enough that the answer was pretty clear. It would have been kind of cute if his fury didn't interfere with our mission and maybe even put our lives in danger.

"Do you remember the pattern that was painted or dyed into the fur of the guinea pigs?" Dave asked.

I blinked. The stupid concussion made me woozy and now my husband had apparently changed the very important subject that I didn't consider closed by half.

"Huh?"

"In the lab when we first came here, did you happen to notice the pattern in the guinea pig fur?"

I tried to think. "Yeah, I guess. Something with some dots and a line, right?"

He nodded. Looking around, he moved closer and dropped his tone. "I noticed something today when I put the zombie down on the table. There was a brand or something with the same pattern on it waiting there for him."

"Why are you whispering?" I whispered with a shake of my head.

"*He* might be listening," Dave said, just above a breath, and motioned around the room wildly.

"The zombie?" I teased.

Dave glared at me. "The fucking doctor."

I sat up a little straighter and was rewarded by a burst of pain through my skull.

"So what?" I snapped in reaction to the pain coupled with annoyance at Dave's paranoia. "So he marks his test subjects, it's probably how he keeps track of them. Dudes have done it on farms for years." Oh wait, there weren't farms anymore. "Or...they used to."

Dave leaned in closer. "Okay, then why did that...that *bionic* zombie we saw yesterday have the same marking as Kevin's guinea pigs?"

I stared. "What?"

"It was on his neck," Dave said softly.

I wracked my scrambled brain. "Look, I don't remember anything like that," I said, but I found myself lowering my voice just like he was. Great, now he had me going all covert ops, too. "And if you noticed it yesterday, why not say anything?"

Dave's lips thinned. "When I looked through the sight, I saw some kind of mark, Sarah. I'm not making it up. It just didn't click with me what it was until I saw the brand here today and remembered the guinea pigs."

I shook my head. "That's crazy. Kevin has told us more than once that all his lab assistants were killed during the initial weeks of the outbreak. And he hasn't had any live specimens to work with, that's why he needs us to collect zombies for him. So why would a crazy, jacked-up mutant zombie be running around in the world with his mark on it?"

Dave ground his teeth. "Well, maybe he fucking *made* it, Sarah. Maybe he's been making them all along. He *is* a mad scientist."

I threw up my hands. "*Scientist*, Dave. That's all. You

just don't trust him because you're jealous for some weird reason and because scientists are what started the outbreak. But that's not his fault—"

He stared at me. "Do you *want* to be naïve or are you that badly injured?" he snapped. "I. Saw. The. Marking."

I struggled for an explanation. "That thing was far away and seeing it freaked us all out. Are you sure you didn't just imagine it?"

He backed away even farther, the chasm between us suddenly uncrossable. "I didn't imagine it. I *saw* it."

But I'd looked at that thing for a long time, too. And I *hadn't* seen it. My head was too cloudy and pained to try to figure that one out.

"I don't know," I sighed as I rubbed my eyes. "It just doesn't make sense."

"It makes perfect sense, Sarah," he said, folding his arms and staring at me. "If only you pay attention."

I opened my mouth for what I hoped would be a stinging retort when the door behind Dave opened and Kevin stepped back in.

"I'm sorry to disturb you, but I wanted to check Sarah again," he said with an apologetic smile.

Dave snorted. "I bet you do," he snapped, but he stepped away regardless and let Kevin in between us.

He checked my eyes and took my pulse, his hands cool and clean against my skin. "Better now," he reassured me as he stepped away. "But I'd give it a day or two before you start capturing zombies again. I have two specimens to work with in the interim."

Dave's jaw dropped open like it was on a hinge and he stared at Kevin blankly. "Wait, go back out and catch more zombies?"

Kevin nodded, his own expression just as confused as my husband's. "Of course. I realize there was a little accident today and I can understand how that might throw you off, but I *do* hope you'll continue to bring me infected things to work with."

"You are fucking batshit crazy," David roared, pushing forward.

He grabbed Kevin by the stark white lapel of his lab coat, smudging it with blood and sludge as he slammed him against the door and held him there.

"We *aren't* going out again. I'm done. And she's sure as hell done. We're done."

There was silence in the room for a long moment and then the sound. A sound I knew all too well. The sound of a Colt .45 being cocked between the two men.

And I knew for a fact that Dave wasn't the one holding it.

CHAPTER 13

Partnerships don't last forever.
The zombie apocalypse just might.

I edged over to the end of the bed and slowly found my feet. When I got up, I was greeted with an entire war's worth of explosions of pain in my head and all through my body, but I fought through it. Oh, and also through the waves of nausea that came with it (you didn't want to see beef jerky and breakfast bars come back up, especially *together*, I assure you) and managed to wedge myself between the two men. One thing was for sure, if they made me, I was going to puke on both of them just to teach them a lesson.

Jackasses.

"Stop it," I said, placing a hand on the .45 Kevin held and turning it away from Dave and me. "Stop it *both* of you. You're acting like schoolboys on a playground except the guns are real. Shooting each other will get us nowhere. Don't forget who our enemy is."

"I know exactly who the enemy is," Dave growled behind me. "Mr. Comic Book Villain here. All you need is a thought bubble, asshole."

I spun to face him. "*Stop*," I insisted, grabbing his arms. "I know you think you're right, but you are being crazy. And as much as I appreciate your protection, you *don't* speak for me on this."

Dave stopped glowering at Kevin and instead jolted his face down at me. "What?"

"You told him that *she* isn't going out anymore. But you didn't ask me what I want to do," I said softly.

He stared at me for what seemed like forever, eyes wide and face pale, before he finally pushed my arms aside. "You can't be serious."

I looked at him and then at Kevin, who was smiling slightly, I suppose in support of what I was saying. Or maybe he was just a smug son of a bitch.

"I realize you two have wildly differing views on this, but I do think that what Kevin is working on could change our world," I began.

Dave snorted. "Oh, I totally agree, Sarah. I'm sure all those bionic zombies will change everything once there are enough of them."

I froze in my spot. I never thought he'd go straight at Kevin and accuse him of something so vile. Especially without more proof than a marking he thought he'd seen in the heat of a really crazy, unbelievable moment.

Kevin moved forward. "Bionic zombies?" he repeated, blinking behind his glasses. I noticed now that there were flecks of . . . *something* on them. "What are you talking about?"

"So your major at the University of Crazy was mad science and your minor was bad acting, right?" Dave asked.

I backed up to the bed and sat back down because my head was throbbing.

"Over the past few weeks we've heard reports of a new kind of zombie." I sighed. "Yesterday we saw one for ourselves. They appear to be bigger, maybe more alert, stronger. I started calling them bionics."

Kevin drew back, but after a moment he nodded. "Bionics. And *you* think I created them?"

The question was directed toward Dave.

My husband folded his arms. "I'm pretty fucking certain, actually. Hell, maybe that's why you want us to bring all these zombies to you. Maybe you're making your own little souped-up army."

"And *why* would I do that?" Kevin asked with a humorless laugh.

Dave shrugged. "Maybe you saw too many *Resident Evil* flicks and found yourself always rooting for Umbrella Corp rather than the hot chick. Maybe you like how it feels when you play God with dead things. Maybe you think you can take over the Badlands or even storm this supposed Midwest Wall that everyone believes is out there. I have no idea what your twisted mind would have as a reason to fuck with monsters that are already bad enough as it is."

"David, please," I whispered, although I have to admit, I was watching Kevin for his reaction to Dave's accusations. For now, there wasn't one. All the emotion was wiped from his face and his gaze held steady on my husband.

His hand held just as steady on the .45.

Finally he sighed. "David, you've been in the Badlands, as you call them, a long time. I can't imagine what you've seen and done and been through. And I suppose it's because of those experiences that you have such a low level of trust, such a low level of tolerance for hope. But I promise you, there is no way I would ever participate in making 'bionic' zombies, as you put it. I'm trying to eradicate this infection, not mutate it to my own devices."

"Hm," Dave said without hesitation. "Sounds like something a mad scientist *would* say."

Kevin's eyelids fluttered just a little, his only tell that what David said annoyed or angered him. His voice remained calm, though.

"Very well, you've made your point clear. You have no faith in me. And I suppose none in any hope that this *thing* that has happened to our world can be changed. But what about you, Sarah?"

His gaze turned on me, piercing behind the glasses. I shifted slightly beneath it, especially when I felt Dave's stare with equal intensity and force. I felt like I was being tugged between two worlds.

Dave was the world I could see, the world of today. And you may not believe it, but there was some comfort to that. After all, now I knew exactly what *this* world entailed. After a few months, I understood the whole zombie thing and the camp thing and the survivalist thing. I knew how to endure.

But I wouldn't call it living.

As for Kevin...well, *he* represented a world I couldn't yet see. A future world where maybe zombies wouldn't exist anymore. Where maybe there was hope of getting back to what we had all lost. It was all very shadowy and unclear so far, this world he painted for me. And terrifying because I had no idea what would happen if we managed to get ourselves to that new reality.

But that thing, that ideal this man represented...it was *hope*.

"I-I want to believe that what you say could happen... is possible," I admitted, trying hard not to look at David from the corner of my eye.

It didn't work. I saw the betrayal on his face. The pain that I would take some other man's side over his. My heart hurt as much as my head as I dipped my chin and stopped looking at him.

"Then will you stay?" Kevin pressed. "Can I depend on you to keep helping me?"

I looked up. This was it, my last chance to back out. My last chance to keep things status quo. Only I knew I would regret that choice. Especially if somewhere down the road Kevin *did* find that cure. I would always regret not taking a stand to save this world.

I nodded. "Yes. I want to continue helping you."

Dave sucked in a breath beside me and I finally forced myself to look at him straight on. I owed him that much. I wished I hadn't. Beneath the bruises, his face was pale, his eyes almost dead as he stared at me.

I reached for him, but he backed out of my reach.

"Please," I whispered. "Please stay and help me."

He shook his head. "No way, Sarah." His voice was as soft as my own. "I'm not going to help him bring down this world. And I'm certainly not going to watch him bring you down with it."

"Dave?" I said, the sound almost not carrying.

He didn't answer. He just turned on his heel and left the room without looking back. Without saying another word.

"David?" I called again. "David!"

But he was gone.

*   *   *

I guess on some level I thought he would come back. I mean, so he left, but he was a hothead. I figured he would drive around that afternoon (although I hadn't really thought about the fact that he had no vehicle now that our van was toast) and maybe even go into camp for the night. But then he'd cool off. He'd come back.

But he didn't. As I watched the sun rise on the monitors in Kevin's lab, there was no David on them. Not even a hint of him or where he was or what he was doing or if he'd ever bother to return.

I blinked to keep tears from falling and looked around. I was on my own for the first time since the outbreak. Really for the first time in years before that. Even at our worst, Dave had always been there. I hadn't ever been truly alone.

Until now.

Behind me, I heard a door open. I turned to watch The Kid enter the viewing room. He glared at me in accusation. It kind of reminded me of my own dirty looks for my mom when she and my dad got divorced when I was just a little younger than the boy before me.

"Is he back?" The Kid demanded without preamble or explanation of his question.

I shook my head. "No. Not yet."

I looked at him. He was clean, at least. Even his clothes were new, so I guess Dr. Barnes had gone all out and found each of us something to wear (or maybe from the stock here in the lab). Dave's set sat untouched on the chair in my room. Accusing me as much as The Kid's expression.

"How's your arm?" I asked, motioning to his wrapped wrist.

He moved it a little and cringed slightly. "Sore," he admitted. "But I'll get over it."

I turned back to the monitors, my thoughts back to David. "Yeah, me too."

"So he's not returned, eh?"

This time it was Kevin's voice at the door and I turned once again to face him. He was holding a tray, but from my angle I could tell what was on it.

"No, I'm afraid not," I said softly.

"It's too bad, but I suppose each of us has to make a choice in life," he said as he put the tray down.

I stared at what was in front of me. Eggs, bacon, coffee. A croissant. A motherfucking croissant! That was it. I had died in the accident and this was heaven.

"Holy shit," I burst out as I grabbed for the pastry first. "What—what?"

He smiled. "Well, it's amazing what one can do between military rations and other supplies. Please do enjoy." He turned toward The Kid. "You too."

The boy leapt forward without waiting for a second invitation and dug into the food with gusto. With a shrug, I joined him. The two of us ate non-stop for a few minutes before I glanced up to see Kevin watching us. Well, watching *me*. That was enough to make me self-conscious and I grabbed for a napkin to wipe my face sheepishly.

"Sorry," I said. "It's been a while."

He smiled as he sat down in one of the rolling chairs near mine. "No worries. I like to see a woman eat with such passion."

I blushed as I sipped my coffee. "My head is still a little foggy this morning," I said as a way to change the subject.

Kevin nodded. "Yes. Today you'll probably be a bit off-kilter still, but I'm betting you'll be feeling more yourself tomorrow."

I frowned. I hated to put it off that long, but there really wasn't much of a choice. Not without my partner. I sighed. "I don't think I should go out to hunt until I'm well."

"I agree," he said instantly. "Regardless of what your husband thought, I *don't* want to see anyone hurt in the name of my research. Take the day to rest and rejuvenate and we'll see how you feel tomorrow."

I nodded. "It's going to be more complicated since I'll be hunting alone."

The Kid's head jerked up at that. "What do you mean alone?"

I shot him a brief look. "Alone. Definition: without other people. E pluribus by-myself-us," I chuckled. "And you say you like to read."

The Kid glared at me without acknowledging my little joke. "No way. I'm going with you."

I stared at him. "Robbie, your wrist is going to slow you down. You can hardly hold that cup, let alone fire a weapon or tie a knot."

"So how the hell are you going to catch one by yourself?" The Kid asked, filled with brimstone and righteous indignation that was almost laughable when it came in child-size.

I shrugged but I turned my gaze on Kevin. "Dr. Barnes here is going to give me *plenty* of his knock-out juice and a way to shoot that shit from as far a distance as possible."

Kevin hesitated for a fraction of a moment, but then he nodded. "Of course. I *have* been working on a dart gun for future use in dispensing my cure, should I ever perfect it.

I'm sure if you give me today to work on it, I can adjust it to fit your purposes."

I nodded slightly. "And there's one other thing you'll do for me today."

His eyes widened and I was pretty sure a dirty thought had just crossed his brilliant little mind. I ignored it as best I could.

"And what is that, Sarah?" he asked, his pervy tone proving what I'd just guessed.

"I want to see this place," I said softly. "*All* of it."

He stepped back. "What? Why?"

"Just because I decided to stay and fight your little battle doesn't mean I don't have my own doubts about you," I said through gritted teeth. "Dave brought up more than a few good points about why we shouldn't take you at face value. So before I go off to be your lackey again, I want to know what I'm working for. Exactly."

There was a moment of shuffling and Kevin sent a slow side stare at The Kid, who sat with his arms folded, looking at the doctor like he was ready to fight to get me what I wanted if it came to that. Which was sort of cute, really. But finally Barnes nodded.

"Very well, if you insist," Kevin sighed. "I'm happy to show you the lab, though I doubt it will be very interesting to you."

I got to my feet, grabbing my half-full cup of coffee and the last bite of my croissant as I moved. "Oh, Doc. I'd be willing to bet good money that I'm going to see more than enough to keep me interested."

CHAPTER 14

The seven habits of highly effective
zombies. Hint: Most of them
involve eating your brains.

It turned out Kevin was right. His lab was pretty boring, actually. The Kid had been right in refusing to come along on our "dumb adventure." Now I kind of wished I'd gone to take a nap like him. But here I was and I was determined to stick to my plan. It would make Dave proud to see me questioning the good doctor's facade...even if he wasn't here and maybe never coming back.

Since it had originally been a military facility, there were several observation rooms where privates had sat once upon a time and watched the television monitors for...I don't know, whatever they thought was going to threaten the facility, I guess.

I'm thinking they didn't have "zombies" on that list. Or maybe they did.

There were plenty of storage areas, too, stacked high with weaponry and equipment for a very long, very bad disaster (kind of like the one we were in). But I'll admit, none of the supplies I saw shocked me. None screamed,

"Secretly making bionic zombies, planning to kill you all! 😵"

On one side of the lab, there was a kitchen and a mess hall. The kitchen still functioned (as proven by that morning's culinary delights), but the mess hall was dusty and empty. Apparently Kevin took his meals at his desk like every good overworked employee should.

"You *really* ought to get out more," I laughed as he closed the mess hall door behind us.

He shrugged with a grin of his own. "I've heard there's a lot of new sights in the world. But most of it isn't worth seeing."

"That's true," I said with a sigh. "But maybe we can change that."

There was a moment's hesitation. "Yeah, maybe. If we do, perhaps you can be my tour guide upon my triumphant return to the world."

I cast a quick glance at him out of the corner of my eye, but didn't respond. He'd been sort of half-assed flirting with me for the past half-hour. The worst part was that I sort of liked it.

Oh, don't judge me. I wasn't about to take him to one of the labs and latch him down on the table to have my way with him. But it was nice to be *flirted* with a little. In a post-apocalyptic world, you kind of end up missing whistling construction workers and inappropriate comments at work that get everyone sent to sexual harassment classes. It's a normal part of life and when it's gone you notice.

We turned down one of the many halls in the labyrinth of the lab and started to steer by a few closed doors. Kevin moved past me, whistling slightly as he maneuvered me toward another area, but I didn't follow. Instead, I came to a stop.

"And what's in here?"

He stopped in the middle of the hall and slowly pivoted on his heel to face me. "Er, lab rooms. Testing facilities. We're mostly storing equipment in them now. It's nothing you'd want to see, Sarah."

I arched a brow at his reluctance. Maybe Dave was on to something with his mad scientist statements after all.

"Please don't make me regret giving up my entire life to stay here and help you," I said softly as I motioned to the door. "Open it."

Kevin let out a put-upon sigh, but he did as I asked and swiped his key card through the scanner. Immediately the door popped open to reveal . . .

Nothing. Just an empty room with some equipment pushed to the far back wall of the area. I smiled with relief.

"See," Kevin said with a knowing shake of his head. "Boring."

"Still, I'd like to see more, thanks," I said as I motioned to the next door.

He arched a brow. "Losing faith, Sarah?"

I frowned. "No. Just not losing my head over what very well might be pipe dreams."

There wasn't any more discussion as he started unlocking doors. One after another, he proved himself correct. They were just filled with supplies like food and medical items, paper and printer cartridges. After seeing about ten of them down two different hallways, I had to cry Uncle.

"Okay," I said as he moved to the next door in the seemingly endless line. "I give. You're right. Your lab is boring as hell. Don't show me one more room of toner cartridges and cleaner fluid."

He chuckled. "Well, then let me take you on the truncated tour, instead. Just the highlights, eh?"

I laughed as I followed him, this time ignoring the shut doors he passed as we turned left and right, left and right until we reached the same hall where we had put the first zombie we caught for him a few days before. At least, I *thought* it was the same hallway. Honestly, the design of this place was meant to confuse. I guess just in case some fool stumbled in here with an agenda.

He opened the door in front of him. A dark room greeted us, the silence of it only punctuated by the faint ping of some kind of a machine. He reached in and clicked on the fluorescent lights and then motioned me inside.

I was right. There on the table where we'd left him a couple days before was our first captured zombie. I recognized him from the hash marks on his face where he'd given himself rope burn on our first net. He almost looked like a rotting body with a soccer ball head now. Cute.

The thing was latched down to the table, oozing body covered in a sheet that was spotted with sludge stains. One bare, gray arm was laid out over it, black veins bulging against rotting flesh, and an IV was pressed into his skin. His eyes were open, red and dead, but he was still, not thrashing around or trying to eat or escape.

He didn't breathe. Well, not in a traditional sense, anyway. He took in a lungful of air about once a minute or maybe ninety seconds. He never exhaled.

"God," I breathed as I inched closer. "What did you do to it?"

Kevin scurried forward, the thrill and pride in his eyes undeniable. "These are the effects of the special sedative I created."

My brow furrowed. "I-I thought you said earlier that the zombie we brought in yesterday was the first one you tested it on."

He turned toward me slightly and there was a fraction of a second of hesitation before he said, "I gave the sedative to this one yesterday *after* you brought yours in. I wanted to see if I could mimic the same results. My research has really only just begun. I'll need to test so many things on these specimens."

I nodded, though I wasn't fully satisfied with his pat little answers. "So have you given him the curative treatment yet?"

Kevin shook his head. "No, not yet. The sedative seemed an important item to test before I had too many zombies on site. If I'm not able to control them, things could get out of hand far too quickly."

I shivered as I flashed to the accident. I was starting to recall more and more of it with every passing hour and I sort of wished I could go back to my blank memories. Actually, that feeling when I woke up and thought this entire zombie apocalypse was a dream was pretty good, too. Maybe Kevin could make me a serum for that sometime. If he put it on the market, he could make a mint.

I smiled at him. "Well, I can't wait to see the results once you start using the cure on them."

He returned my expression, but there was something troubled in his eyes that I couldn't help but notice. I tilted my head slightly.

"What is it? You seem worried."

He shifted. "Do you know me so well already, Sarah?"

Now it was me who shifted. "I don't know about that. You don't hide your emotions very well for a scientist."

He laughed and the tension between us faded a little, thank God.

"It comes from being away from people for so long I've forgotten the niceties and politeness involved in everyday interaction," he explained. "There isn't anything wrong, per se. I only worry that you may be disappointed once you see the cure at work."

"What do you mean?" I asked, wary.

He shrugged. "While the guinea pigs did respond well and integrated back into their society after the cure was administered, the human brain is far more complex."

"Obviously," I said. "At least in most cases."

"Indeed." He chuckled again. "But with those complications that make us so...*human*, I can't say for sure that the zombies will fully return to normal. Those who are freshly infected may be perfectly fine. Those who have been gone for a long time may die instantly or even turn into mindless drones. I have no idea what will happen in the long term."

I reached out to grab his hand and held it for a brief moment. "Kevin, no one is asking you for the perfect solution here. I certainly don't expect it. But if there were a way to turn even a small portion of these people normal again or prevent the freshly bitten from turning into monsters, my God, why not try it? And I much prefer mindless drones to killing machines, I promise you that."

He looked down to where my hand touched his and I followed his gaze. Instantly, I drew back and stepped away from him. He smiled.

"You are a very interesting woman, Sarah," he said softly. "The fact that you haven't lost all hope, become completely jaded by all you've been through, is amazing."

I looked down at the zombie on the table, but I was thinking of David. He was jaded. He had no hope left. Or at least that's what the doctor believed, what we had both accused him of before he stormed off the previous afternoon.

Except now that my anger had passed, I couldn't really believe that accusation to be accurate. David had always fought with everything he had to survive, and even harder to keep me safe and alive.

If he had truly lost all hope, why would he even bother?

"Since you're going to be field testing the sedation formula for me, I'd like to show you how and where I administer it," Kevin said, his voice pulling me from my thoughts of David.

I nodded.

He touched the zombie's head, eliciting a soft mutter from it that caused me to reach reflexively for the gun I normally carried in my waistband. It wasn't there, of course, since I was in the lab, and for a moment stark panic overwhelmed me. My heart began to race and my mind conjured images of this *thing* rising up. There would be nothing I could do.

Kevin reached out and his cool hand touched my arm. "It's okay, Sarah. I promise you, he isn't going to wake up any time soon. They still mutter and moan in this state, just as we do under sedation."

I nodded as I forced myself to calm down. Or tried

to, anyway. Freaking out wasn't going to help anyone. Though that had never stopped me before.

"Sorry," I whispered as I motioned toward the zombie again. "Show me."

Kevin released my arm and used both his hands to slowly turn the zombie's head away from me.

"You see here," he said, indicating a small puncture mark on the side of the creature's neck.

I nodded as I stared, but I wasn't really seeing the needle mark. No, instead I couldn't help but look intently at the *other* mark on the zombie's neck.

It was a brand with three circles and a line. Just like the one on the fur of the guinea pigs we'd seen less than a week ago.

Just like the one David had described to me on the bionic zombie. I stared at it. He'd said it was on the thing's neck. And here was another of Kevin's zombies...with a brand on the exact same spot Dave had told me about.

"Do you brand them all?" I asked past dry lips.

Kevin nodded, although he seemed briefly annoyed that I had interrupted whatever it was he'd been saying while I zoned out.

"Yes. I try to mark any creature I'm working with so that I can easily tell which ones I've tested on and which ones I haven't. Also, in case they escaped my care, I would be easily able to identify them for recapture."

I nodded as he began to explain about shooting the dart into the neck so that the serum didn't have to work so hard to reach the brain, but the uneasiness in my chest persisted and kept his words from completely sinking in.

No, this didn't prove anything. After all, Dave had certainly seen the marking before on the guinea pigs in the lab. And I was still stuck on the fact that I *hadn't* noticed the brand on the bionic. It was entirely possible the situation was just as I had accused Dave of creating. He'd imagined the marking because he didn't like Kevin and didn't trust his work.

I backed away a little further. "Well, that all makes sense," I said with a little nod. "I'm certain I'll get it all figured out once I have the dart gun in hand."

Kevin's brow wrinkled as he watched me move away from him. "Is everything okay, Sarah?"

I nodded. "Oh yes. Just tired."

He shook his head. "How stupid of me. Of course, you must be exhausted. Enough time has passed since the accident that if you'd like to lie down and get some rest, it would be safe. I'll monitor you before and after."

I forced a smile as I allowed him to lead me to the hallway and back toward the room where I could sleep. As much as I tried to convince myself that there was nothing to be worried about, my thoughts nagged at me. I doubted I'd get much of the sleep I so desperately needed.

And if I did, I couldn't imagine that my dreams would be pleasant.

CHAPTER 15

Dress for success. Also arm yourself for it.

By the time the next morning came, I actually felt a lot better. My head was no longer foggy and a long day of rest (my first since the outbreak happened) had done me more good than I'd thought it would.

I had even managed to purge myself of most of my doubts about Dr. Barnes after many talks and explanations of his behavior, mainly to myself, but sometimes with The Kid shrugging and "I dunno"-ing at my side.

Helpful, that one.

Now Kevin and I rode up the elevator together. The Kid wasn't with us. He was still pouting over being left out of my hunt for the day and refused to speak to me, even to say good-bye. So it was just us. Alone.

I looked in his direction as we passed from the bright lights of the lab area up into the darkness of the chamber that would eventually lead to the warehouse above. As the green and red lighting system buzzed past I could see the tension around his mouth and eyes.

"Are you sure you'll be okay alone?" he asked as the platform reached the top and the door above us opened to flood the area with sunshine streaming in from the holes and collapsed section of the warehouse roofing. It was kind of pretty, really, as the light caught on the dust.

I nodded. "I'll be extra careful."

"I could come with you," he offered.

I looked at him in his stark white lab coat and his crooked glasses. Sure, I knew he could handle a weapon to some extent, although I'd never technically seen him fire anything except for the remote guns and there wasn't a whole lot of aim involved in that. Somehow I couldn't imagine a scenario where he would be more help than harm.

Unlike Dave, who could always be depended upon when the going got tough.

Plus there was the little problem that if Barnes got hurt or killed or turned, there would be no one left to further develop his curative serum. Any future without zombies, at least any future I could see at the moment, would vanish along with Kevin's mind and body.

"I have the tranq liquid," I reminded him with false cheer as I lifted up the dart gun he'd provided for me just an hour before. "And there's always the big cannon to use in a bad pinch."

I frowned and looked off into the distance toward the lonely road that led out of here. "As long as Dave didn't take it from the van when he left, that is. I'll be fine."

I didn't feel fine thinking about the hunt without my partner in crime and life, but there was no point reiterating that to the doctor or myself.

"Speaking of the van..." Kevin began as we walked out into the sunshine.

I stared as he motioned his arm toward a big SUV parked right in front of the warehouse. It was a little banged up and dusty as hell, but it had a huge frame mounted to the front for pushing other vehicles around and was more than roomy enough in the storage area for a zombie, maybe even two.

Plus, it was way better than our van, which I now saw flipped on its roof over on the side of the road. The driver's side was almost entirely caved in and I forced myself to look away and not think about what exactly that could have done to my body if I hadn't been lucky as hell.

"What in the world?" I gasped as I hurried toward the new vehicle.

Kevin clicked the automatic lock button on the clicker in his hand and let me open it up.

"It was one of the ones left parked by our staff in a warehouse just behind ours," he explained. "See, I *do* get out occasionally."

I flung open the back hatch of the vehicle and peered inside. This was a full-sized model and there was almost the same amount of room as you found in the beds of some small trucks. The carpeting in the back was stained, it looked like with blood and dust, but at this point, that was commonplace.

Plus, whoever had run with the vehicle before had installed one of those roof-to-floor divider guards that kept cargo from the back from falling into the seats in front of it. I wasn't sure how long the flimsy metal would hold a zombie when tested, but it would certainly keep me safer from one should the sedative fade while I was bringing the beast back to Kevin.

"I put all the weapons I could find from the van into the back seat," he explained.

I moved around and opened the passenger door behind the driver's side. Sure enough, a big collection of my weapons and ammo were stacked neatly on the back seat and the floor, including the cannon I'd so coveted.

From what I could see Dave had only taken a few weapons and enough ammo to get him out of the area. He would have to resupply soon if he didn't intend to come back to find me.

God, I hoped he was okay.

I blinked against weirdly sudden tears and slammed the door. "This is great, thanks so much."

Kevin stepped toward me, his face intense and still filled with something more than simple friendly concern. "Just stay safe out there, okay?"

I nodded as I got into the front seat. He handed me the keys, his fingers lingering just a moment too long on mine before I got them and was able to close the door between us.

I rolled down the window. "Look," I started after a second's hesitation. "If something *does* happen to me, I have a couple of friends who might be able to help you. And also take care of The Kid—"

"Friends?" Barnes looked confused.

"Yeah." I shook my head. "I mean, I might be hurt or worse and I'd hate for it to stop your progress. These people I'm talking about, they have hunting experience. The guy was apparently a chemist at some point. Their names are Josh and Drea, The Kid met them a couple of days ago—"

Barnes's eyes went wide and he burst in to interrupt

me. "No, *no*! Just be careful. Be careful and everything will be fine."

I nodded even though what he said was anything but true. I started up the engine and waved as I pulled away from the warehouse, leaving him in my rearview mirror, just watching me go.

I clicked at the stereo in the hopes that there might be a CD in the changer to fill my brain with something other than thoughts of Dave and the obvious crush Kevin had on me.

The sound roared forth from a decent set of speakers. Damn, it had been a while because we'd been driving that ancient hulk of a van for so long. The CD in the changer was Alicia Keys. Nice.

As she sang to me about New York (did it still exist?) and lost loves and played out all her passion on the keys of her piano, I tried to relax and mentally prepare myself for what I was about to do.

I already knew a couple of things. First, I had to be on my best game. Fighting zombies alone was a huge risk, catching them alone... well, the idea of it danced dangerously on the edge of suicidal. But I'd basically given up my husband for this choice of a hope for the future. I wasn't about to back out of it now and make that awful sacrifice be in vain.

Second, I wanted to snag a female zombie. Kevin had two males on his tables in the lab rapidly disappearing behind me, but a woman's chemistry was different and I wanted him to be able to test his serums and theories on a wide variety of subjects.

Settled with those goals in mind, I drove onto the highway, but I have to be honest and tell you, I had no real plan in mind. And trust me, running without a plan is always a bad idea in the zombie-infested Badlands. Without one, you might as well just hang out a sign on the side of your car that says, "Eat me."

And not in the way the women who sold themselves at the camps for food did. Gross.

But I plowed forward anyway, maneuvering my car until I found a school. Why a school?

Okay, so sexism says that more teachers are female than male. Lots of zombies stay in the general area of their origin. Plus, the school was in what was once a residential area. There had been lots of zombie chow here in the beginning, I'm sure.

So with all that in mind, it followed that within the walls of...Creekside Elementary (a ridiculous name since we were in the desert with no creek within any reasonable distance to the school), there were probably a couple of chicks still roaming their classrooms, hanging with the students who they had turned or who had turned them one fateful afternoon just before recess.

I pulled into the parking lot and took a space right near the door even though it said HANDICAPPED.

Here's a weird thing. Even though parking wasn't exactly at a premium in the last few months, I still felt really guilty about taking a spot meant for someone disabled. I mean, my great auntie had owned a handicapped placard because of some weird hip thing and every time I slid into one of those extra-wide spots with the little blue chair in it, I could hear her screeching voice in my ear, repeating her favorite phrase:

"For shame, Sarah!! For shame."

Today was no different and I muttered, "Shut up, Auntie Rose," to myself before I looked around me.

There were a handful of rusted-out cars in the lot and a sludge-covered bus parked half up on the sidewalk, both good signs that *someone* had been home when the plague hit the school. I pulled my supplies from the back seat and began to load up as I played potential scenarios out in my head over and over.

Dave always told me I needed to think more and act less on emotion, and he was right. As always.

Today more than ever, though, his advice was spot-on. He wasn't there to protect my ass so I had to be very certain that I was ready for all contingencies before I took step one into the dark, low building that had once been a place of learning and children's laughter.

The dart gun was vital, so I took it. Also the bat Dave had created for me just a short time ago. I admit that putting it into place at my utility belt made my heart hurt a little. I missed the goof. A lot.

And then there was the cannon. I hadn't actually tried it out yet, but it wasn't too complicated, especially for someone as well-versed in weaponry as I'd become. Funny, back when this started, I had no clue how to shoot and could hardly reload. How quickly things change.

But anyway, the cannon was basically a big-ass gun that could fire hundreds of bullets at once, spraying down any target (or targets) in a few presses of the trigger mechanism.

The only problem was that it was a *huge* thing. When I strapped it across my back, my knees actually buckled a little from its weight and I had to readjust all my other supplies (including the rope to bind whatever I hoped to catch) before I dared move forward into uncharted and dangerous territory.

Still, within fifteen minutes of pulling into the lot, I felt ready enough to start toward the big double doors that led into the school building.

Heading up the long sidewalk that led to the entryway, I was struck by a feeling that this was all so familiar. I could almost hear the soccer moms at the curb, yelling out directions to their children as they scurried through the yard. I could almost see the teachers herding little groups of kids toward the front of the school as the bell rang to signal the beginning of the day.

When the infection had come to the school, what had brought it? Some little latchkey kid who no one cared enough about to notice he'd been bitten by someone? Or a rabid janitor who was already kind of weird so no one noticed until it was too late? Maybe even a stuffy principal whose morning announcements that day had been *very* different.

I shook away my thoughts and tugged at the doors, but I found they were locked. It didn't really surprise me.

When the shit started going down, there was no way the schools hadn't gotten a "lock down" order. You can thank Columbine and other school shootings for that. It was just standard operating procedure meant to limit the *incident* as much as possible.

Only in this case, once the people in this place were locked down, they were also locked *in* with whoever and whatever had already been infected. At that point, I could well imagine all hell had broken loose amongst the kids with ADD and the teachers who were already burned out and waiting for retirement. Once they started turning on each other...

Well, it must not have been pretty (although maybe a tiny bit satisfying for some of the teachers).

I could only hope someone had managed to get out alive. Maybe somebody like The Kid. He was about the right age to be ending his elementary career and moving up to the junior high down the street. Smart kids like him had some kind of advantage, at least.

I reached through the already broken glass and turned the bolt from inside to get access.

The hallways were wide and had probably been well-lit at one point. I had somehow picked a school district that actually had money, because there was very little wear on the floors or walls.

In fact, staring at the happy signs and fresh paint, one could almost picture that school was just about to pick up at any minute after a good, long summer break. Kids could have just walked back in around me and started learning and fighting and breaking up into cliques.

Except for the fact that there was a dried blood pool three feet across at the base of a staircase straight ahead and black sludge smeared across every door down the hall, of course.

Yeah, I had definitely come to the right place. There had been activity here at some point. And judging from the wetness of some of the sludge, recent activity at that.

"Hey zombies," I murmured softly as I eased through the halls.

They were still decorated with WELCOME BACK! signs. See, the initial outbreak had started right in the middle of August, so these rooms had been prepared for new students with new dreams.

New problems, too. Bigger than budget cuts or the increasingly unprepared student.

I stopped at one of the classroom doors. It said 2B, MRS. PEEPLES on the door. A perky little paper sun smiled down from near the placard, sunglasses perched on his round little sunshine nose. Tempered, fogged glass covered a big portion of the door, I guess to keep the kids from being distracted by stuff in the hall. Unfortunately, it also meant I couldn't see shit inside. Still, there was no obvious movement from within to warn me off.

Slowly, I gripped the doorknob and turned it. Unlike the front door, it opened easily. No locks for classrooms, I guess. Inside, I looked around. Though there was a mustiness in the air from the room being locked up for so long, the familiar and comforting scent of chalk and glue still lingered in the background, taking me back to my own childhood.

Sun streamed through the big windows. They were filthy with sludge, both outside and more tellingly, in, and caked with sand from three months' worth of dust storms, but they still provided enough light that I wasn't totally blind. I glanced around, scanning for the teacher, even for a little kid who would make a good specimen. It may sound awful, but if it meant ending this, I'd probably take in my own mother.

The mother I currently hoped was safe behind what might be a mythical Midwest Wall.

"Mrs. Peeples," I called out in the dusty air. "Time to come to class."

Behind me there was a screech of a chair being pushed and I spun to face the sound. The door I'd opened then glided shut and standing behind it was who I assume might have once been Mrs. Peeples.

She was wearing a long, really *ugly* jumper-type dress that I think once had a Winnie the Pooh sewn appliqué of some kind on the front, though it was mostly ripped off with only half a honey pot and part Winnie's little yellow leg left behind (fitting in a zombie world). Beneath it, she'd once worn a yellow t-shirt of some kind, but it was turned brown and smudged from the months of devastation.

She'd been sensible and worn little Keds with ankle socks, probably so she could chase her class around outside at recess, but sometime over the intervening months, the little thin soles had worn off, leaving her mostly barefoot.

"Gross," I whispered as I shuddered at the sight of her dirty, bloody toes.

Some things are still yucky to me. Feet are one of them, okay?

I guess my commentary must have offended her, because Mrs. Peeples bared her teeth with a grunting roar in a tiny little voice that was almost cute except it signaled a real desire to deal death and undeath.

I yanked the dart gun from across my back and aimed just as she started toward me in a jolting, dragging speed walk. Her arms flailed around her almost like they were disconnected and her head turned sideways as she sniffed for me as these things often did.

I pulled off a shot and the dart entered her neck exactly where Kevin had told me to place it. She kept moving forward, one step, two steps, three...

Bam!

She teetered forward, her red eyes rolling back in her head, and then collapsed down on the ground between the mess of little desks that had been tossed about during the outbreak.

I stared down at her, totally silent and unmoving. Had I killed her? Had the fall killed her? I mean, zombies are half-rotten, so they often die from head blows that would only give a regular person a hell of a headache. That's one of their few weaknesses.

I set the dart gun down and instead pulled out my 9mm. Holding it with one hand, I grabbed the zombie's shoulder and flipped her on her back. She stared up at the ceiling with open, blank eyes.

"Not dead," I said with a sigh.

See, they were still red. When a zombie dies their pupils go blank and black. They don't stay red. Red means alive and wanting your flesh.

I stared down at the living corpse. Now I just needed to get her from the classroom to the vehicle. She was light enough to carry, but I wasn't sure I trusted the sedative enough yet to just sling her over my shoulder and hope she didn't wake up halfway down the sidewalk.

I pulled the rope from my belt and carefully bound her arms at her sides. I'd watched The Kid make his special "Boy Scout" knots about a dozen times, but I still wasn't so great at it. When I tested them, though, they seemed like they'd hold for a while, at least.

Still, I wasn't sure how to carry her. Dang, this was easier when I had Dave around. He could have taken the feet, me the shoulders, and we would have been loaded up already.

But he was gone and I had to do this alone now.

I sighed and looked around. Immediately, my eye was drawn to a cart in the corner of the room. It was covered with paint jars and other supplies and was probably normally used to disperse those things to the kids for art class.

Today it was going to disperse me a zombie.

I grabbed it and pushed it over to the body on the floor. In one satisfying sweep of a forearm, I threw the paint and other things onto the floor. They clattered and banged, sending sprays of yellow and blue and red across the once pristine white tile.

Yes, there is *some* fun in being in an apocalypse. You do get to play at being an avant-garde artist sometimes. For instance, the stain across the floor was a part of my Blue Period, kept forever for posterity (or until someone covered it up or the building fell down).

With a chuckle, I grabbed the zombie teacher and flopped her up over the cart on her stomach. She hung awkwardly, her feet almost touching the ground on one side and her dirty hair swinging against the floor on the other.

I got behind the cart but it wouldn't roll no matter how hard I pushed. With a curse, I bent to check the wheels. There was some kind of locking mechanism on the dirty, damaged metal that only allowed them to turn in one direction and no matter how much I pulled on it, it was rusted in place. With a sigh, I switched sides and began backing the cart toward the door.

I edged into the hallway, with my zombie making occasional little breaths in and me grunting from the effort of pulling the cart around with dead weight. Oh and also, the burden of her body kept the fucked-up wheels from spinning freely. Basically it was a clusterfuck, but it was the best I could do.

I cursed as the back wheels caught on the divider between the classroom and the hallway and started to tug, slamming the back wheels against the low edge again and again. The sound echoed in the empty halls, *thwack, thwack, thwack!*

And then the *thwack* was joined by another sound. *"Ehnrrrr!"*

I let go of the cart, pulled my 9mm out, and spun toward the loud burst of nonsensical sound.

"Oh fuck," I whispered.

My gun started to shake. Standing at the end of the hallway were two zombies. Little kid zombies in uniforms. A boy in short khaki pants and a white dress shirt, and a girl in a khaki skirt with the same white shirt.

They were filthy, covered in sludge and sticky blood. The girl zombie's face had half rotted off, revealing some of the teeth beneath her cheek. The boy's arm was gone at the shoulder and he hunched unnaturally in the other direction, like he couldn't adjust to the misbalanced weight.

Remember that scene in *The Shining* with the twins where they want the little boy to play with them? Forever.

Yeah, I was having flashbacks, especially when both of them turned their heads sideways at the same time and sniffed the air together.

I turned to see if I had an escape route the other way, but what was at the other end of the hall was actually worse. Three zombies. One normal zombie, probably another teacher, judging by the brightly colored soccer ball tie he had once worn. It was now just a knot at his throat with tattered threads at the end (the shirt collar that had once held it was long gone).

But the other two were something different. Not children, not normals.

These two were bigger and they had a brightness to their red eyes that spoke of some kind of remnants of intelligence.

These two were bionics.

CHAPTER 16

Building relationships is building business.
Also you sometimes need other people in order
to kill all the motherfucking zombies.

I swiveled from one side to another, but all my mind could think of was, *now what?* Dave's voice echoed in my head with the same thing he always said to me when the going got tough.

Stay calm.

I drew a deep breath and leveled my 9mm at the little kid zombies first.

What? They're smaller and easier to take care of. Also, I was fucking terrified of the bionics and I wanted to just ignore that issue as long as I could.

Of course the second I pulled off the first shot and dropped the little girl zombie, the little boy started jogging toward me. Behind me the other three roared with blood (er, *brain*) lust and as I spun toward them, they started after me, too.

"Shit!" I shouted as I made for the classroom I'd just left.

Unfortunately, the cart with my unconscious teacher zombie was half-blocking the door and I couldn't close it. The closed door wouldn't offer me much protection, but at least it was some kind of barrier between me and the attacking group that now gathered at the entrance, staring at me, turning their heads to the side like confused dogs.

All three regular zombies, including the child, ignored the cart and just started crawling over it to get to me. On top, my unconscious zombie chick whined in protest about the extra weight squashing her back . . . literally. But the zombies didn't care, zombies never do, they just kept reaching out toward me, grunting and groaning.

But the bionics were different. They hesitated at the cart, staring at the unconscious zombie, then looking past her at me. I'm not going to say that their eyes reflected really clear thoughts on what I was doing . . . or even what they should do in response, but fuck man, they were certainly a lot more lucid about the situation than the others.

I backed up against the wall as I stared at them staring at me. The windows were behind me and beyond them the yard and escape, but they were the safety kind of window that tilted in so that the kids who were all amped up on sugar wouldn't crawl out during class. By the time I figured out the safety releases, I was pretty much fucked.

The two bionics looked at each other now. The one in front had to crane his neck a little to do it and when he did I sucked in a breath of shock. The world slowed to half time and all I could do was stare.

There, on his neck, was a brand. Three dots and a line.

Kevin's mark for his zombies.

I could hardly believe it and I shook my head like it could clear my eyes. But the mark was still there, bright red and tinged with black against the gray, rotting skin of the zombie's neck.

Seeing it proved everything Dave had been saying to

me all along. He *had* seen the brand on the other bionic a few days before. And Kevin had fully admitted to me that he marked his specimens with the thing.

So if both those things were true, Kevin...*Dr. Barnes* had made these horrible things. And he'd looked me right in the eye and lied about it.

He really was a mad scientist.

Even worse than that, when the bionics started shoving the biting, growling normals out of the way and began to move the cart to clear a path to me, I got a better look at the bionic in the back.

He had long, stringy hair that fell over his face, wild, wide eyes that bugged out just a little, and dirty clothes, but they weren't rotted away by weeks or months of lack of career. He was a fresh zombie, bionic or not. And an all-too-familiar one, at that.

"Jimmy No-Toes," I said out loud.

He jerked his head up almost like he recognized the name, but then he went back to pushing the cart. Finally, the two of them got it over the lip of the door and shoved it with all their considerable strength. The cart flew out of the way, crashing against the desks in front of me, and cleared a direct path to me.

I lifted my handgun and fired off three shots in rapid succession. Even shaking, I got all the normal zombies right between the eyes. They crumpled in a big pile while still in the doorway, but the barrier of their bodies didn't slow the bionics down. They just stepped over them and started toward me in a steady, flat-footed walk that kind of reminded me of Drago in *Rocky IV*.

I could almost see one of the bionics saying, "I must break you."

Oh and they would, too. No fucking doubt about it. That was what they were made for.

I shot again, but my hands were shaking so hard that I only winged the front zombie (Non-Jimmy) in the shoulder. He growled as he looked down at the wound and then back to me. Okay, so that had apparently only irritated him. Shit.

I pulled for the cannon on my back, expecting it to pull free as easily as my shotgun always did.

Yeah. Not so much.

It was so heavy that it took a fraction of a second longer than I'd expected. And that fraction of a second was enough time to allow the front bionic to launch into a sprint.

I screamed as he bore down on me, but I somehow managed to barely dodge his attack by diving to my right. He smashed into the windows where I'd been standing a moment before. His heavy arms shattered what was left of the glass and sent the metal frame spiraling across the room like a deadly boomerang.

Well, there was a way out now, but a fucking monster blocked it, so not much help there. I raced for the back of the room, hoping I could get the two hideous beasts to follow me and clear a way to the door. All the while I worked to get the damn cannon from its sling across my back, but it was just so awkward.

I spun around to see if my plan was working. Fuck no. The Jimmy No-Toes bionic hadn't come inside like a normal zombie would have. He was waiting for me at the door, his stringy hair hanging over his once ratlike face as he growled at me. The other one was right behind me, herding me like a lamb to the slaughter, I guess.

I was boned. This was it. There was no way out. Panic overtook me and I had the strangest urge just to dive under the closest desk and cover my eyes like we had done during earthquake drills in school.

But before I did something so foolish, there was the loud burst of shotgun fire from the hallway. Bionic Jimmy's head exploded like fireworks in front of me, his black-tinged brains spraying across the room and raining down around me before he fell forward and thudded to the floor.

I didn't have to be asked, I jolted for the escape route and whoever had been my savior.

"Human!" I screamed as I burst blindly into the hall. "Don't shoot!"

Dave stepped out of the doorway of a classroom across the hall. He smiled at me as I skidded to a halt and stared at him in utter shock.

"I have no intention of shooting you, babe." His eyes widened as he looked past me. "Unless you don't move!"

I dove for the floor, flattening out as I skidded across the hall toward him on my stomach. His shotgun exploded again, echoing in my ringing ears at such close range. As I flipped around, I watched as the Non-Jimmy zombie collapsed forward into the hallway, most of his face gone from the shotgun blast. He hit the linoleum with a thud that reverberated all the way to me and then lay still.

For a long moment Dave and I were both silent, just staring at the carnage before us. And then I got up and threw myself into my husband's arms.

"You came back," I sobbed, not even aware I was crying until I felt the wet from his shirt against my face.

"Of course I did," he said, holding me tight. His heart was throbbing just like mine. "I wasn't about to let you get hurt. Once you got on the highway, I followed you all day today. I would have followed you for the next year if I had to."

I pulled back and looked at him. He was beautiful and dependable and whole and *mine*. And I owed him a big fucking apology. And probably a blow job or something, because I had truly screwed up.

"You were right," I said as I swiped at tears and pulled myself back together.

"I can never hear that enough," he chuckled.

I didn't laugh with him. The situation was just way too messed up. "No, I mean you were really, *really* right. The bionics *do* have that same brand as Kevin's, just like you said they did."

His smile faded and he looked at the dead bionic in the hallway with a deep frown. What was left of the creature's head was turned away from us and even now I could see half the brand on his neck.

"They *did* come from his lab, David," I whispered as I turned away from the proof. "He did make them, or at least he *knew* they were out here rampaging. And he lied straight to our faces about it."

Dave blinked. "I sort of hoped I was wrong," he finally whispered.

I stared at him. "You did? I thought you hated Barnes."

"Not Kevin anymore, is he?" Dave asked with an arched brow that made me blush.

I shook my head. "Asshole, prick, freakazoid...but not *Kevin*, that's for fucking sure."

"Well, I *do* hate him," Dave said with another slightly smug smile. "But that doesn't mean I wanted what I said to be true. There was some part of me that hoped maybe he really did have everyone's best interest at heart. That we really did have a prayer of ending this shit."

"Hope, huh?" I asked as I took his hand. "I thought you didn't believe in that."

"Nobody's perfect," Dave laughed. "Now, where's The Kid? I think it's time for the three of us to pick up and go to new pastures. Barnes will be looking for us as soon as he figures out we know his secret and I'm sure as hell not delivering any more new lab rats for him."

My eyes went wide. The Kid!

"Oh Jesus," I said, pacing away from Dave down the hall. "The Kid, oh Christ, The Kid!"

"What?" Dave asked, staring at me. "Is he hurt?"

"No," I shook my head. "Oh God, I don't know. He isn't with me."

Dave's mouth dropped open. "Not with you? Why isn't he with you?"

I sucked in a gulp of air that hurt my chest. "He-he was still hurt from the accident. His wrist...I thought it wouldn't be safe to take him when he might not be able to handle a weapon or fight off a zombie. So I..." My voice dropped to a whisper. "I left him behind. W-With Barnes."

Dave covered his face. "Shit, oh shit. He's back at the lab? He's alone with that fuck face?"

I nodded as the tears I'd shed earlier came flooding back to my eyes. "Oh my God, David. That bastard was going on this morning about needing new specimens, ones of all types. He must want kids, too. He could do anything to Robbie. He could hurt him, he could test horrible things on him...he could *kill* him if he wanted to without us there to protect him."

"Shit," Dave whispered. "We have to get him."

I was about to nod but before I could, the sound of a rifle action sliding into place cracked through the silence of the hallway. Both Dave and I turned slowly to face the sound.

My first reaction was relief because standing before us was The Kid himself. The only problem was that he was holding a rifle...and it was aimed at us.

"Robbie," I mouthed.

"Hey," he said, his tone completely normal and even sunny. "You know you two don't have to worry about me. I mean, my dad would never do anything to hurt me. But he does want me to bring you back to his lab." He slipped the safety off the rifle. "Now."

CHAPTER 17

Rich dad, poor zombie.

Your dad?" Dave repeated, just above a whisper.

Robbie nodded solemnly as he held his rifle steady on us.

I shook my head. So Robbie had lost it. That was okay, it happened all the time out here.

"No, honey." My tone was ultra gentle. "You're just confused. He's not your dad."

"Oh yeah, he is," The Kid insisted without an ounce of hesitation.

I stared at him, then looked at Dave. "I-I don't understand."

"Who do you think left the note in the camp for you?" The Kid asked before he motioned toward himself with a finger he lifted briefly from the rifle. "And why do you think I just *happened* to show up and lead two zombies right to you when you couldn't get your own the first day you were hunting for him?"

Dave swallowed hard. "Then why didn't you just tell

us who you were then? Why did you act surprised about the warehouse and the elevator and the electric lights and all that shit?"

"It was all part of that sick fuck's game," I whispered.

Robbie nodded again. "He wanted you to do what he wanted. And he needed someone to watch you. If you knew I was doing that, you wouldn't have been so... honest."

"You little punk," I snapped as I reached for him.

His finger tightened on the trigger. "Please don't make me shoot you, Sarah. I like you. I don't want to hurt you or kill you."

I stopped. At some point I don't think I would have believed Robbie would pull the trigger. Now I didn't know anything anymore. Turns out I was a shitty judge of character, as my choices of friends clearly indicated. At least friends in the Barnes family.

There was a bang off in the distance that sounded like desks being turned over and all of us looked toward it.

"Sounds like all the shooting brought some zombies from the upper floors," The Kid said, watching us with a wary side glance. "So we should probably get a move on before they come. Grab your specimen."

"What specimen?"

He tilted his head. "The lady on the cart, Sarah."

I stared. "You knew I got one? You watched me?"

He nodded. "Of course. I had to follow you to make sure you were doing what you were supposed to do." He glanced at the dead bionics in the classroom doorway. "Dad's not going to be happy about that, though."

"Son of a bitch," Dave grunted through clenched teeth.

Robbie shrugged. "He has his reasons. I'm sure he'll

explain them if he feels like it. Now grab the woman and let's go."

Dave and I looked at each other briefly. I think we both were thinking about defying him, maybe even trying to disarm him, but I'd seen The Kid fight. One or all of us could end up dead that way.

So we climbed over the bodies, took the unconscious zombie off the cart and let The Kid walk behind us as we made our way to the SUV parked outside.

"Keys?" he asked mildly, just like it was any other day with him.

"In my pocket," I grunted.

He shook his head as he slipped his little hand inside my pocket and grabbed them. As we moved around to the cargo hold, he shook his head.

"No, I think you two are more dangerous to me than she is in this state. So why don't you put her in the back seat and you two can sit behind the gate in the cargo area."

I shook my head as he unlocked the vehicle.

"Robbie," I said, trying to keep my voice free of the anger and betrayal I felt. "You have no idea how long that shit I gave her will last. She's been out for almost half an hour already and she could—"

"Two hours," he said as he motioned with the gun for us to put her in the backseat.

"What?" Dave said.

"She'll stay out for almost exactly two hours unless I inject her again." The Kid smiled but there was a hint of pity in his stare, too. "Come on, Sarah. You know my dad lied to you about a bunch of other stuff, do you *really* think he hasn't tested *all* his stuff on the zombies like hundreds of times?"

I blinked. Of course he had. But if that was true, why had he needed us? I guess I'd have to ask him the second I saw the fucker.

We slung the zombie into the back and propped her up against the opposite door. At Robbie's insisting, we even buckled her in.

"What are you going to do, use her to ride in the HOV lane?" Dave asked with a shake of his head as we closed the back door.

"Maybe," Robbie laughed. "Wouldn't want to get a ticket, right? Now, you two get in the back. It's unlocked."

I exchanged another look with Dave. "You could tell him we just got away," I said softly. "You'll have his zombie, right? Why not just let us go?"

"We've been your friends," Dave encouraged.

There was a brief moment of guilt that flashed in The Kid's eyes, but then he shook his head. "But he's my dad. I have to do what he wants. Just get in."

"Fuck," Dave grunted as he climbed into the back of the SUV.

I clambered in after him, but before I could get settled, Robbie said, "Now sit back to back. I'm going to tie you up."

"What?" I started, but Dave grabbed my hand and gave me a look. The Kid would have to put the gun down to tie one of his fancy knots, which just might give us a chance for escape.

Except . . . he didn't. He pulled a handgun from one of those many magical pockets of his and leveled it in my face as he set the shotgun down at his feet. Keeping it steady, he somehow managed to get ropes wrapped around both our wrists and a knot tied.

All with one fucking hand.

"Damn, kid, you really are good at that," I said with begrudging respect.

He smiled as he started to put the back door down. "Well, there's not exactly a lot of TV to watch anymore. I have lots of time to practice."

Then he was gone, the door shut and the two of us trapped behind the cargo gate. I rested my head back against Dave's shoulder.

"So now what?"

"I don't know," Dave sighed. "I'm thinking. Aren't you supposed to be the brains of this operation?"

I laughed despite our situation. "Well, let's see, I believed a mad scientist and a crazy kid over you. I'm going to say that my brain power isn't so great anymore. I may already be a zombie."

Dave's fingers found mine and he squeezed gently. "Just stay calm. We'll figure a way out of this."

I wasn't so sure as The Kid got into the SUV and put it in gear just like he did it every day.

"Are you really eleven?" I called forward in the vehicle as he squealed the tires out of the parking lot and steered us back toward the highway.

"Yeah," he called back. "That part was true. Why?"

"Well, you're fucking driving the car like you're in the 500," I said as Dave and I rocked helplessly as he took yet another corner on all but two wheels. I think he might have been getting even for all the times our driving threw him around in the back of the van.

"You should have seen me following you on the motorcycle earlier today," The Kid said with the smugness of a child who has the coolest new toy before anyone else. He smiled at me in the rearview mirror, but his eyes barely appeared in the glass because he was so short.

I blinked a couple of times at the idea of such a thing. "*You* know how to drive a motorcycle. At fucking eleven years old?"

He rolled his eyes. "I learned how to drive when I was eight, running around in the desert while my dad worked in the lab."

Behind me, Dave shifted. I could feel his rage, his betrayal, bubbling through his body. It made his back hot against mine.

"It's okay," I whispered.

He craned his neck back a little in a jerking motion. I could only see a tiny portion of his face from the corner of my eye as I strained toward him, but he looked as pissed as he felt.

"Well, I guess we'll find out in a minute," he said. "We're pulling up to the warehouse."

I craned my neck. Sure enough we were. And who was waiting for us? Barnes. He waved as The Kid slid into place in front of the old building and put the SUV in park.

Robbie got out and closed the door behind him. We couldn't hear them, but I watched in surprise as The Kid approached Kevin. The doctor opened his arms and embraced the little boy briefly, ruffling his hair as they parted. They spoke for a moment, with The Kid motioning occasionally toward us and the car.

Kevin's smile eventually fell and he walked up to the back of the SUV. Slowly, the hatch back glided open, sending a stream of bright sunshine in to blind us since we couldn't lift our hands to shade our eyes. Barnes stepped in front of us, though, and then he blocked the sun, becoming only an ominous shadow standing before us.

"Hello, Sarah, David," he finally said as he leaned down so I could see his face. It was remarkably smug. "I do hope you'll forgive my boy for bringing you to me this way. But this has become our only option, I'm afraid."

"Fuck you," Dave spat.

Kevin smiled slightly, though the slur made his eyes lose a bit of their pleasure. Apparently he still didn't like the language, which made me want to sing any song I could think of from *South Park* if only to piss him off. "Robbie's Dad is a Bitch" seemed like an appropriate alteration of one.

"Let's all go inside, shall we?" he said with a gesture toward the warehouse . . . like he was inviting us in for fucking tea or something.

He pulled out a shotgun of his own (aw, matching father/son psychos, how cute) and motioned us out of the car with the barrel. Since we were tied, exiting the SUV took some maneuvering, but we finally managed to slowly move out of the back of the vehicle together. Back to back, we walked toward the warehouse.

Dave was in the lead, facing forward. He never dragged me, in fact we were almost in perfect tandem. Those facts made me feel more guilty than ever about not believing him . . . about taking the side of the son of a bitch who walked behind us, that smug smile still trained on me as he cradled the shotgun in his arms. How had I ever thought he was even remotely cute?

The Kid was in front, leading the way. I could hear the soft crunch of his boots on the gravel up ahead of us and could only imagine that poor Dave was just keeping it together having to follow the little brat.

We should have just let the damn zombies eat him back when we first found him. But hindsight is twenty-twenty, right?

Down the elevator we rode and let me tell you, *that* was an awkward ride. I'm sure you know what I mean. Haven't you ever gotten on an elevator with just a couple of people, maybe even one of whom you know a little, but no one has anything to say? And it feels like it takes forever to get to your floor?

Yeah, it was just like that except with guns and bound hands. Oh and no elevator music, thank God.

Still, we somehow made it into the lab and as the doors downstairs opened, Dave shook his head.

"What the fuck with all this captive shit, Barnes? If you're going to kill us, why not just get the fuck to it?"

I jerked to look at him over my shoulder. Was he nuts? I mean, I hadn't fought for so many months just to get shot with my hands tied behind my back like some kind of mob moll in a bad *Godfather* rip-off. At least I wanted the *chance* to fight.

"I don't like waste, David," Barnes said as he stepped closer to us. "I like to use and re-use. This *will* be over for you soon enough. At least, I think it will be."

"What do you mean, you *think* it will be?" I asked, hating how my voice shook.

He looked at me and there was a tightness, a sadness around his mouth. "We may know a great deal about how the zombie body functions, but very little about the mind. For all I know, those poor souls are utterly aware of everything going on around them, their minds intact and unable to stop themselves as they dive into their victims and roam the earth in rotting hell."

I squeezed my eyes shut at the nightmare Barnes painted. My stomach turned and I barely kept my food from earlier in the day down. I really wished I hadn't eaten his crappy croissant.

"Now, move," Barnes said, the softness in his voice gone as he pressed the side of his gun against Dave's chest and shoved him.

Dave snapped forward with a rather feral snarl, dragging me behind him as he rolled up on Barnes.

"Hey!"

All of us stopped and turned because it was The Kid who had spoken. He held his gun level to Dave's face and he said, "Let's just go to the room and we'll talk this all out there. Okay?"

Dave was tense as a board as he shook his head in disgust, but he followed The Kid, forcing me to back along behind him, my eyes once again on Barnes.

"Is he your real kid or is this one of those 'New World-New Family' deals you see so often in the camps?" I asked with an even glare for Barnes. I still couldn't believe they were related, no matter what Robbie said.

He stared back at me evenly. "Oh, he's very much of my own flesh," he said with a smile. "Don't you see it in our eyes?"

I shook my head. "I guess I never looked closely enough."

He nodded. "Well, that was your mistake, I suppose. One of many I'm sure you're reviewing in your head right now and kicking yourself for them."

I didn't get to respond because we moved into a room. This wasn't a place I had seen during my tour of the facility the previous day. But then, as Barnes had said, that had been my mistake, too. I had been willing to believe that what he showed me in those first dozen or so rooms was true and had never guessed that it was all a manipulation. He'd made the gamble that I'd give up when so many rooms he showed me were anything but sinister.

Stupid me, his bet had paid out at least double. But then, I'd never done so well in Vegas anyway.

The room was big, with bright lights above that made the sterile white walls all the more painfully stark. I blinked as I looked around. There was a big window on one side of the room that looked into a lab. On the other walls were large doors, but they didn't look like they opened on hinges, but rather slid up and down.

Barnes backed up to the door and lifted his shotgun to his shoulder. "Now, Robert, please do untie Sarah and David. And don't try anything, you two, because I *will* shoot you without hesitation."

I bit my lip, glaring at the doctor as The Kid unlooped the ropes around our wrists. Once we were able to break apart, Dave and I turned to face each other, each rubbing our raw wrists and looking at the other. There was no need to say much, we'd been together long enough to read something of the other's mind and mood.

Neither of those were filled with very positive thoughts. As the door we'd entered slammed shut behind Barnes and The Kid, I reached out to take Dave's hand. I shook my head.

"Sorry. This is my fault."

His brow wrinkled and he stared down at me. "Not likely. The only one at fault here is that prick and his brat. They were the ones who preyed on your desire to find some kind of hope in the future."

I dipped my chin as heat flooded my cheeks. "Yeah, well, so much for that, huh? I mean, I should have stuck with your way and only trusted what I could see around me. See where hope got me? *Us*?"

"Hey." He lifted my chin with his finger. "I *like* that you have hope. When you believe there's a future out there…it kind of makes me think that maybe there could be. There can only be one cynical jerk in this partnership and it's me."

"Very sweet," came a voice from the speakers that were mounted around the room.

We both looked at the big window that faced into the adjoining room. Barnes was now sitting at a desk behind the glass, holding a microphone as he stared in at us.

"Where's The Kid?" I asked.

"Still worrying over him even though he's entirely capable of taking care of himself?" Barnes asked, and I thought I detected a hint of surprise in his tone. "He went out to collect the specimen you caught for me, Sarah. And by the way, thank you for that."

"Thanks for almost getting me killed with your freak machines, asshole," I snapped as I took a long step toward the glass.

Dave caught my arm and held me steady so that I couldn't waste my energy going for the window.

Barnes shook his head. "I didn't actually intend for my…what did you call them?" He seemed to ponder for a moment. "Oh yes, I remember now, *bionics*. I like that name. But I didn't intend for my bionics to attack you in the school. I had hoped to drag our partnership out for a while longer before you learned the truth. Perhaps even to find a way to convince you to come around to my way of thinking."

I burst out a grunt of disgust and turned my back on the glass.

"Sarah, if you did decide to join me, we could be a remarkable team," his voice continued behind me. "You are like a warrior woman from some extinct tribe. Think of what we could do with my brains and your brawn and, may I add, beauty. What do you say? Join me?"

I spun around to face him. "I would rather gnaw my own arms off."

His brow arched through the glass and then he shook his head. "Well, it may come to that eventually, I'm afraid."

"Aside from wanting to fuck my wife," Dave snapped as his hand came to rest at the small of my back protectively, "what the hell are you thinking, Barnes? Were you involved in the zombie research? What the hell are you doing creating bionics?"

Barnes settled back into his chair and steepled his fingers in front of him.

"I wish I *had* been involved in the initial research. I'd heard about it, though it was deeply classified. But there are always whispers in the scientific community. But the research was in Seattle and I wasn't able to get a transfer. They kept me here, working on other war elements. Like making soldiers stronger. Faster. More obedient."

I blinked. "Making them bionic?"

"In a way." Barnes shook his head. "What I told you about the plague hitting the city and us being in lockdown was true. When the alarms went off, though, I insisted that Robbie be brought down to the safety of the lab."

"And what about his mother?" I asked softly.

"Let the bitch rot," he snapped, his anger brightening

his face in a rare display of his emotions. "She was sleeping with some army major anyway. A real man, she called him. I enjoyed watching her try to claw her way into the facility."

"Wait, you *watched* her?" Dave asked in horror.

"Of course. I let her see that the boy was taken down to the labs. She begged the cameras, she pleaded with me... but I let the infected swarm over her. She was so torn apart, she didn't even re-animate."

I backed away from the window a step and stared. "Sadistic bastard."

He shrugged. "Vengeance is commonplace in a world such as this. Are you saying that since the plague broke out you've never just killed someone because you didn't like them? I mean, there's no way you wouldn't get away with it."

"There's been enough killing to last me a lifetime," I said with a deep breath. "I don't need to do it to frivolously satisfy my pride or my sense of moral outrage because someone took a parking place from me once."

"Interesting that you compare stealing a parking place to stealing a wife," Barnes said softly. "Either way, once she was dispensed with, the remaining survivors had to deal with the reality of our situation. And when one of the military men became ill, we realized that the infection had been brought down into the lab."

I stared for a moment at Barnes and then let my gaze move to David.

"The infection came down here and you survived?" he asked in disbelief. "In this tight environment?"

"Well, we caught the man very quickly and confined him. In truth, his condition became very useful, for I was able to study him. I took core samples of his tissue, his brain, and using those I was able to begin work on various elements of the infection. One by one, I tested my theories first on the infected soldier, but then I needed to expand my research. So I picked others in our group of survivors."

I covered my mouth. "So these people were trapped down here with you and you used them as guinea pigs."

"No," he said evenly through the speakers. "I used guinea pigs as guinea pigs. I used humans as test subjects. There were a few who caught on to my schemes, but they were easily isolated and taken care of. By the time the power generators went out above and unlocked the elevator, all that were left were just Robbie and me."

"Then why did you need us?" I asked with a shake of my head. "Why call us here and ask us to catch you zombies if you were capable of creating and testing on them on your own?"

He shrugged. "I have created them and tested on fresh and actively turning specimens, yes. But what I told you when we first met was also true. I needed more zombies of differing kinds and rot levels."

"Why not get them yourself?" I pressed. "You're clearly more than capable."

He sniffed like the idea was beneath him. "I wasn't about to go out myself and try to capture them. So you truly were doing me a service by helping me run my tests and increase my ... what did you call it, David? My Undead Army."

I winced because let's face it, this was my fault. Dave never would have gone along with Barnes's request if not for me and my insistence that we try to save the world.

"How many were there down here to start with?" Dave asked. "Alive before the outbreak."

"Ten," Barnes admitted without hesitation.

"So you killed eight people?" Dave breathed.

"Well, seven," Barnes said, unapologetic and even *bored*. "The first one was infected before we were locked down."

I paced to the corner of the room. "And Robbie saw all this? He knows you murdered his mother, that you slaughtered these people?"

"He's eleven, Sarah, I know better than to expose him to such things. That's how people become serial killers." Barnes shook his head. "No, I protected him from all of that, kept him safe from what was happening around us. And the fact that only the two of us survived the lockdown actually brought us closer together. He needs me and loves me just as a good son should. A fact I think you saw demonstrated today."

Dave swiped a hand over his face. "And what if we tell him what you did?"

There was a moment's hesitation. "Why would he believe you over me, his father?" Barnes asked.

"He's a smart kid—" I began.

He turned his attention on me immediately. "Oh no, Sarah. Robbie tested in the top one percent on all the standard I.Q. tests. He's a genius, not *smart*. But he's a boy. And I doubt you'll sway him to turn on the one remaining parent he possesses."

Dave turned toward me, catching my arm so that we faced away from the speakers and the window. "He's probably right. We have to focus on ourselves now. If we can get to The Kid, fine. If not, well, I'd like to live and stuff."

"I doubt that will be an option," Barnes's voice came from behind us.

"God, I'm really starting to hate that guy," I said through clenched teeth before I faced the window. "Okay, jerk-off. So you have us, you don't want us to let anyone else know about your little mad scientist lab, we have no recourse, what's the plan?"

Before he could answer, the door behind him opened and suddenly The Kid reappeared at his dad's shoulder. For a brief second, he looked at us through the glass, then he turned away. He whispered something to his father.

Barnes nodded. "Very good."

I kept my gaze on Robbie. Although Barnes was right that it would be almost impossible to turn The Kid on his only surviving parent, Robbie didn't look very happy at the moment. The fact that he couldn't even bring himself to look at us gave me a little hope.

And maybe it was time for him to grow up and know *exactly* what his dad did to people who didn't fall in line behind him. Whether that got us out of this or not, it might save The Kid down the line.

"So you're going to kill us?" I pressed, moving up to the glass so Robbie would be sure to see me. And I could see him. He flinched. "How? Gas us? Shoot us?"

Barnes's face jerked to me. "Nothing so barbaric. Now Robbie, you may return to your chamber if you'd like."

"No, why not let The Kid know what you're going to do to his friends?" I leaned against the glass. "If it isn't going to be barbaric, then tell me what humane means you're going to use to get rid of us and keep us from going against your desires, *Dr. Barnes*?"

He stared at me through the glass. Our faces were less

than a foot apart. He was angry, I could see that. And I could also see he was pretty much just on the edge of losing it.

"Today you killed two of my bionics," he said softly. "Not very good for my army's record. I want to test them again."

Dave rushed to my side. "Is *that* really what you think you've created? Look doctor, you can't control these things. They may have more purpose, more drive, than your average walk-a-day living dead, but they can't be controlled. If you don't stop this now, they'll turn on you. They'll wipe out whatever's left of the survivors."

"I guess we'll see," Barnes said softly. "Worst-case scenario, you two will kill them and I'll get to hone my skills at creation and keep testing them on *you* until they do destroy you. Best-case scenario, they turn you immediately and I end up with two new specimens and one sticky problem solved. Either way, I win, don't I?"

From behind Barnes, Robbie shifted. "But —" he began.

Barnes spun on him. "What is it?"

"I-I thought we were going to keep them alive," Robbie said. "I thought you said—"

"They're too dangerous," Barnes said, grabbing The Kid by the upper arms and tugging him closer. "They're a threat to us, Robbie. And in this world, we have no choice but to eliminate threats."

"Like your mom," Dave said next to me. "And all those people down in the bunker with you. It seems like everyone else in the world is a threat, huh Robbie? Ever wonder when you'll become one to him too?"

Barnes glared at David. "Shut up," he snapped. He

turned back to The Kid. "Now *you*, go to your quarters if you haven't the stomach for what must be done. *Now*."

The Kid stared at his father for a brief moment and then his gaze moved to us. And there was one thing very clear to me when our eyes met. Robbie was afraid. Afraid of his father, afraid of everything that had happened since the outbreak. On some level, he knew what was happening here. He knew it wasn't right.

But he didn't argue. He didn't do anything except turn around and leave the room without so much as a backward glance for us.

My heart sank. He was our only chance for someone on the outside to help us. Now that he was gone, our options had faded out to just about nothing. Fight or surrender. And there might not be much choice there, either.

"You see," Barnes said as the door closed behind his son. "With a little discipline you *can* raise an obedient child even in a post-apocalyptic world. I should write a book."

"You do that," Dave said quietly. "I'd love to read your thoughts on raising a man."

Barnes's face fell at the implication of my husband's statement, and when his smile returned it was a harder, colder expression.

"Well, this has been fun, but it's time for testing. Enjoy." And then he reached across the desk and depressed a button hidden somewhere beyond my line of sight.

CHAPTER 18

Profits aren't everything. If you can get out with only your ass intact, that's pretty good, too.

The three doors on the walls around the permeter of the room began to slide upward in tandem. I clenched at Dave's arms as we watched the open space increase to reveal feet, legs...yeah, *zombies*.

Three zombies, to be precise, who rushed the room as soon as the doors cleared their rotting skulls.

And of course these weren't normal zombies, either. I mean, that would have been bad enough, but these were bigger. Broader. Two of them I recognized as the ones Dave and I had collected earlier for Barnes. The third was dressed in the tattered remains of a military uniform, so I had to assume he was a much older friend of the "good doctor."

Whoever they had once been, wherever they had come from, they were all but foaming at the mouth as they stared at the two of us, unarmed in the center of the room. They were all bionic zombies.

"They're worked up," Dave said softly as we shifted to stand back to back. "He's given them something."

"Excellent observation," Barnes's voice came from the speakers. "You're correct that they've been drugged. I'm testing a new mixture to raise their intent to fight. It's harder to rouse them than you might think."

"Harder to rouse them!" I cried.

The military zombie dragged his leg behind him as his rotten lips curled back over black teeth. He was missing an eye, too, the open socket just sort of gaping at us. But the one that still existed watched me with rabid intent.

"Indeed. Now ... I suggest you fight."

The speaker crackled off and there was no longer any background reverberation, so I had to assume Barnes had shut the system off so he could just watch our struggle in silent satisfaction.

"Remember the last kung fu movie I made you sit through before the shit hit the fan?" Dave asked from behind me.

I fought the urge to turn and stare at him and instead kept my focus on the snarling zombie still moving on me from the door. Black drool leaked from his waggling tongue and pooled at his feet like oil from a dirty engine.

"You want to fucking talk to me about Jackie Chan movies right now?" I asked, my voice cracking.

"No. I want to talk to you about killing zombies without weapons," Dave responded through clenched teeth. "There was a move in that flick that involved two people back to back like we are now. Remember?"

I scanned my brain for what the hell he was talking about. I mean, when you're fighting for your life on a regular basis, you tend to brain-dump a lot of useless shit. Or at least file it under "crap I don't need." But then like a shot in the dark, I remembered.

I looped my arms through his.

"This isn't going to work," I whispered.

"I know," he said and then he lifted me up and started to spin.

I was wearing heavy boots and the first zombie I kicked got the steel toe right to the temple. He whined as he dropped down to one knee, half his rotting head caved in.

I would have probably taken more time to celebrate that fact, but Dave was still rotating, steering my flailing feet toward the next zombie. This one was too far away for me to catch his skull, but I did manage to press the bottom of my boot into his chest.

It sunk in a couple of inches and when I tugged to free myself, some flesh came with me as the zombie staggered backward toward the wall.

That left Sergeant Ugly, but by the time Dave made the 360 degree turn, the military bionic was already right up against us. As my boot came around to find a home in his side or his neck, he reached out and he caught it.

For a moment all of us stopped...or maybe it just felt like that because it was so fucking creepy. But there we were: Dave was looking over his shoulder. I was staring at the zombie. The zombie held my ankle and was staring right back at me. The frozen feeling might have lasted a second or ten minutes, I don't know, but when it ended, it ended with a bang.

The zombie tugged and I slipped out of Dave's grip. I slammed down on the floor on my back and the wind went out of my lungs as my head, still hurting from the concussion by the way, slammed on the linoleum. Dave pivoted instantly and threw a punch, but the military zombie dodged.

Yeah, you read that right. He fucking dodged.

With a moan, he tugged and I slid across the floor toward him. That woke me up and I kicked upward with my opposite foot. It caught him right between the legs and the zombie's eyes widened just a fraction as he whimpered ever so slightly.

He flung my foot and I twisted into a half somersault and hit the ground again, this time on my stomach. Pain ricocheted throughout my chest, vibrating through my entire being as lightning exploded in front of my eyes.

Still, I fought through it, trying to find focus again, trying to remember that we were talking life and death here. I could whine about my owies later.

I managed to get up to my knees and then staggered up just about the time the second zombie I'd hit pushed himself from the wall and started after me.

I left Dave to deal with our uniformed friend and headed toward the other bionic with all my weight. We slammed back against the wall a second time and the zombie leaned down, his snapping jaws just missing my ear as I twisted out of the way.

I wrapped my hands around the back of his neck and joined them together in a tight, interlocked fist. Then I thought of every MMA fight I'd been forced to watch by my husband and tugged the zombie's head down with all my might.

He bent at the waist with the weirdest whining screech and I threw my knee upward with all my might. It connected with his forehead and there was a wet squishing sound as the skin exploded against my jeans. Instantly I felt the wet sludge seeping through the cotton fabric. I threw the knee again and the bionic's head caved beneath the force of the blow.

I let him go and backed up as he collapsed forward, face first on what used to be the clean floor, but was now far less stark.

I spun around. Dave was grappling with the military bionic. The two of them staggered around the room together in almost a dancelike fashion. I'm sure *Dancing with the Zombies* will be a big hit once we all get television back.

Admit it, you'd watch it.

I would have rushed to Dave's aid at that point, but the grunting moan to my right stopped me. The first zombie I'd hit, the one whose head was half caved in, was starting to get up.

I stared in utter disbelief at what I was seeing. Normally once you broke any part of their brain, zombies were pretty much toast, but this one could clearly still function only partially intact. The brightness was gone from his stare now, but the bloodlust remained.

I dodged as he swung one clublike arm toward me and staggered in my direction. He was really pissed now, if a zombie could feel such a thing, and he still had pretty good speed even with only half a brain.

I glanced around the room as I dodged a second attack. It was barren, devoid of anything that would even remotely pass as a weapon against the hideous creatures bent on our destruction.

In short, we were fucked. I mean, even if we got past these three sweethearts, we were still locked inside this room, just waiting for Barnes to use us in another "test" of his minions.

So not only did we have to kill these fuckers, but we had to get the hell out of Dodge. And fast.

The zombie lunged for me and this time I couldn't quite get out of the way. He hit my shoulder and the two of us fell back. The window where Barnes was watching took the brunt of our weight and as I sucked in for air and grabbed for the zombie's shoulders, I heard a sound.

The sound of glass being strained. It was faint, but it was there. And it gave me an idea.

I shoved back, sweeping my feet against the infected beast's legs, which sent him staggering wildly. I shuffled to the side and his sludge-y, brain-leaking head smacked the glass a second time. This time, in the corner, a hairline crack appeared.

Barnes must have noticed it, too, because through the glass, I saw his eyes widen. He backed up and stared, first at his zombie, who was trying to claw his way back up to his feet against the slippery barrier between them, and then to me.

I smiled at Barnes and then took off across the room, hoping the bionic would follow me. He spun around, this time slower as his body and brain became more and more damaged by my attacks, and faced me. For a moment he wobbled and I held my breath, hoping against hope that he wouldn't keel over quite yet. I was strong, but I needed his increased weight and power to shatter the treated window.

Finally, he shoved toward me. He moved like Frankenstein's monster as he lurched across the room, one arm dangling uselessly at his side, one reaching for me, clawing at me.

The zombie lunged and I dropped down and slid, face first between his legs. I hit the wall below the window and got to my feet just in time to see the zombie come around like a big, dopey ship. He had woken himself up a little and he lumbered across the room with ever-increasing speed.

"Sarah, don't," Barnes's voice came through the speakers.

Dave jerked his head toward me as he kneed his own zombie in the gut. He stared at me, then at the freight train of a zombie coming my way.

"Be careful!" he cried.

I didn't look at him, just kept my eyes on my prize as it got closer.

"I know what I'm doing," I said and prayed for once I was right.

The zombie staggered and at the very last moment I bolted out of the way. He bent over like an angry bull and his head hit the window at full speed. The impact shook the glass and then the window exploded out into the observation room where Barnes was watching and waiting.

The zombie fell forward, impaled on the glass, his head nearly severed by it, and landed on Barnes's control panel. The buttons all went on at once from the weight of the now-dead body on them and there was a hot smell of burning wiring as the entire thing shorted out. All the doors opened in the room at once.

Barnes stood there for a second, his face pale with shock, his eyes wide. He stared at the carnage around him, then his gaze lifted to me. I couldn't help it. I smiled.

Without a word, he spun on his heel and tore the door behind him open to sprint out into the hallway. As much as I wanted to chase him, I spun away and back into the room where Dave still struggled with the final bionic in our way.

The military zombie was already staggering, his face battered, skin peeling away and skull damaged by Dave's attacks while I was busy dealing with my own problems. As I watched, Dave pulled back to throw a finishing punch.

The zombie's cheek collapsed under the strain and I stared in slow motion horror as my husband's hand disappeared into the mouth of the zombie. And even further horror as the teeth of the nearly dead infected creature closed around his hand.

CHAPTER 19

Do fight unwinnable battles.
Sometimes they're worth it.

No!" I screamed, but my voice sounded far away and odd. It mixed with Dave's howl of pain as the zombie teeth sank into his palm.

I lunged for the zombie, grabbing it from behind by its rotting uniform seams and pulling as hard as I could. Dave's hand popped free from the diseased mouth and the zombie and I fell backward onto the ground. Like a turtle, the *thing* clawed at the air and tried to get itself upright.

But I was faster and up on my feet almost as fast as I was down. With another scream, I slammed my foot down into the zombie's skull over and over again. I relished the feel of my foot crushing away its unlife until there was nothing left of it but a body in a uniform and a splat where its head used to be.

Panting, I spun around to face Dave. He had sunk to his knees in the middle of the room and was clutching his hand, staring at the spot where the zombie's teeth had pierced the skin.

Wounds mean something different when the world as you know it has ended. Because of infection, even the smallest non-zombie-related injury can mean death in the Badlands.

And when it comes to the zombie-related ones, well... there's no difference between having a zombie rip your throat out with his teeth or just barely scratch the skin. You're fucked. You're the living dead.

"I-It's nothing," I lied as I dropped down in front of him to look at the mark.

Yes, it was just a little break of the skin. But already the black edges were beginning to appear around the torn flesh. Telltale sludge was creeping into his bloodstream and making Dave bleed black-red instead of normal.

He looked at me, his eyes wide and steady. "It doesn't matter, Sarah. It's all over."

I squeezed my eyes shut. That was the one truth I couldn't hear. "No. No."

He grabbed my upper arms and squeezed. "It *is*, babe. The best I can do now is help you get out of here before I turn. Then we have to put a bullet in my brain." I opened my mouth, but he cut me off. "You know that's true."

"No!" I shouted in his face.

He grabbed me and tugged me against his chest. I hung tight to his neck, burrowing my face into his skin and biting back sobs as I felt his warmth all around me. Soon there wouldn't be any warmth. Just cold death.

Unless...

I tugged back to stare at him.

"Small injury on a hand gives you about thirty minutes until you change," I said, hardly able to breathe as my mind put together pieces. "And maybe forty if you hold still and stay calm so that your heart doesn't pump the poison through your system as quickly."

"Thirty minutes, forty minutes, what does it matter, Sarah?" he asked as he reached for my cheek to brush a tear away.

"There *is* a cure, David," I whispered.

"It's a pipe dream," he grunted, his voice already strained.

"No! No, it's not. We *saw* it work when we watched Barnes test the guinea pigs. He made a cure, maybe to protect himself and the kid, maybe to just fuck with the zombies, I don't know. But it is here … somewhere. And if I can find it before you turn, I could save you."

"No way." Dave shook his head. "Even if that shit *would* work on me, and there's no guarantee that it would, that asshole is armed by now, Sarah! He's not going to just let you take his cure and come back here to me. And he's definitely not going to let us waltz out of here even if you can find it."

I grabbed his shirt and pulled him close for a quick kiss. "I'd like to see him try to stop me. Now lay here, stay still, and like you always tell me, stay calm. I *will* be back."

He reached for me as I pushed to my feet. As he stared up at me, I couldn't help but notice that his pupils were dilating rapidly. That his skin was getting pale already.

"Sarah, if it takes longer than half an hour, you have to run. Just leave me, okay? Leave me and *run*!"

"I promise," I said as I bolted for the door that had swung open when I blew the control panel in the observation panel.

I lied.

*   *   *

There were guns in the dining hall area and that was close enough to the guinea pig lab that I headed there first.

What? I was crazed, not stupid. I needed weapons since I was pretty fucking sure I was going to encounter Barnes again before this was all played out.

I stared for a second at the key card slot that would allow me in and then kicked it. The mechanism shorted out and the door popped open at the same moment that a high-pitched alarm began to whir over and over again from the speakers strung throughout the hallways.

Ignoring the annoying sound, I burst into the dining hall and grabbed what I needed. Two handguns, ammo. I could have taken a lot more, but I needed to be fast. Five minutes had already bled away from the time left for Dave to stay Dave and I wasn't even close to where I needed to be to save him.

I loaded as I made my way down the hallway, doing my best to remember just the right twists and turns to find the lab where we'd first seen Barnes's guinea pig zombies. Not an easy task considering we'd come to it from a different direction and that on my fake-ass "tour" I'd been suffering a concussion. I broke open more than a few wrong doors before I finally made a last turn down a hallway I hadn't visited yet.

And at the end of it was Dr. Barnes himself, leveling a rifle on my chest.

"You son of a bitch," I growled as I moved down the hallway in long, certain steps, my handgun trained on him evenly. I have to be honest, at that point, I didn't give a shit about getting shot.

"You'd best stop right there," Barnes said, but his voice shook in a rather satisfying way.

I did what he asked and took a quick glance at my watch. Fifteen minutes were gone. Dave had fifteen, twenty at the outset before he'd be gone from me forever.

"Listen to me," I growled, accentuating each and every word. "I *know* those fucking guinea pigs are in that lab behind you. And so is the cure you used on them. And I'm getting it. Even if I have to put a hole in you."

"You want that cure so badly, you'd get shot for it?" Barnes laughed.

"For David, I'd do anything," I snapped. "Just like he'd do anything for me. Unlike you with your wife and your poor kid, I actually give a shit what happens to him. So I would suggest you put that rifle down and let me pass."

He stared at me a long moment, sizing up the situation and working out a judgment of what he thought was going to happen. Finally, he smirked.

"Or what?"

I didn't answer, I merely depressed the trigger and prayed the element of surprise would work for me.

It did. I hit his hand, blowing his gun away just as he pulled his own trigger. A huge hole blew through the wall beside him as his thumb went flying off his hand and bounced down the hallway toward my feet.

I moved down the hall again as he collapsed forward with a wretched howl of pain that didn't nearly satisfy my hatred for him. He wrapped his bleeding hand in his lab coat as he looked up at me.

"You bitch, you blew my thumb off!" he said, stating the obvious in a way that no longer indicated brilliant young scientist.

"You're going to lose a lot more than that," I said as I

trained my pistol right on his groin. "Now tell me exactly where the cure is or I will shoot pieces of you off until you do. And I'll like it."

He stared up at me, making little voiceless whimpers.

"Go ahead, test if I'm willing to do it," I ground out through clenched teeth.

"In the lab," he confirmed. "It's the blue liquid."

"I'm going to bring it out and inject you with it," I promised. "So you better tell me the right fucking one."

His eyes grew wide. "The purple liquid!" he corrected himself. "It's the purple one!"

I smiled and then swung the butt of the pistol back and brought it smashing across his temple. His eyes rolled to the back of his head and he lost consciousness, and slumped in the corner of the hall by the door.

I pulled his key card from his waist and glided it through the reader. The door button turned green and there was the swish of releasing air as it popped open to reveal the dark lab beyond.

I clicked on the light and looked around with a sigh.

The fucker had released the guinea pigs. And they were *all* zombies. They were collected in the middle of the floor, ratlike creatures with glowing red eyes that hissed and growled at me.

Now it may sound silly (and in retrospect, it was pretty ridiculous to have one of the most innocuous animals on the planet standing up on its pudgy back legs and clawing at you), but one bite or even a scratch from these things and I was as much toast as Dave.

I plunged into the room, squashing the little rodents as I went, ignoring their squeals as I stomped them and kicked them across the room. There's nothing like watching a rabid guinea pig go cartwheeling across a room with a little squeal, I'll tell you that.

The purple vial was on the other side of the lab, already attached to a syringe for the robot arms to collect and use to nullify the infection on the guinea pigs. I reached it as the last remaining zombie pig made a kamikaze leap onto my leg. I slammed it away with the barrel of my gun and grabbed the purple serum.

As I ran past Barnes in the hallway, I didn't stop. He'd been too sure I was going to inject him to lie and I didn't have time to see if he was zombiefied by what I carried with me or not. I just had to trust, and pray this was actually the cure.

I ran through the twisting halls and finally found my way back to the lab where Dave and I had fought the bionics. As I skidded into the room, I looked at my husband.

He had managed to drag himself across the room and was propped up in a sitting position on the wall with his hand dangling at his side. A great idea since the blood would have to work harder to infect him. His eyes were shut, though, and I stared.

Was I too late? Had the infection spread faster…there wasn't any standard litmus for the time, of course, just some basic guidelines. Different people, different body chemistry.

"Are you going to give me that, or just stand there and watch me go all living dead?" he grunted without opening his eyes.

"Oh shit," I breathed, my heart finally starting to beat again. I rushed to his side and dropped down with the syringe in my hand. I was just about to depress the plunger when a voice at the door stopped me.

"If you inject him, I'll blow his brains all over that wall."

I turned and found Barnes in the doorway, the bloody rifle I'd shot out of his hand earlier now trained at us again. He was leaning against the frame, his damaged hand still half-wrapped in his lab coat. Not that it did him much good. He was still dripping blood across the floor and the front of his lab coat was bright with ugly red splotches.

"You didn't kill him?" Dave asked, his voice strained.

I looked at my husband. His skin was gray and his lips were starting to tinge black. We had moments, maybe even just seconds before he was gone.

"Let me do this!" I screamed at Barnes. "Don't you want to know if it works on humans?"

The doctor chuckled. "Oh, it does. I've tested it many times before. On both fully infected subjects *and* on those who haven't yet turned. It was the long-infected subjects I hadn't played with yet. Do you know what happens once a person goes full zombie?"

He didn't wait for me to ask.

"It turns out they lose most of their brain cells almost instantly. So if I wait for you to return him to normal until *after* he's become the living dead, then I get to watch you both suffer."

I stared at him. Barnes looked perfectly serious and my stomach dropped. The idea that Dave could be saved, but would still be irrevocably compromised, made my hands shake.

"*Why?*"

"You ruined my research," he said and then he lifted his hand. "And you took my thumb. And I have worked too hard and for too long to give it all up for—"

He didn't get to finish. As he started into what looked to be a long, villainous monologue that wouldn't end until Dave did, there was the explosion of rapid gunfire behind him.

Barnes's eyes went wide with shock and disbelief before he tipped forward and landed face first on the floor. The two holes in the back of his head told the story.

Behind him was The Kid, holding a smoking gun. Tears streamed down his face.

"Fix him!" he demanded, motioning to Dave with the barrel of his gun. "Hurry!"

I jammed the needle into Dave's arm and depressed the plunger. He sucked in his breath and stiffened beneath me. His head began to twitch and he grimaced as whatever I'd put into him moved through his bloodstream.

The Kid lowered his weapon and we both watched. Waited. Finally, Dave opened his eyes. And they were green, not black. Not red. Not filled with a desire to overtake and feed.

"Hey," he said, and his voice was normal, not strained anymore or garbled by growing infection.

"Hi," I whispered as I moved toward him.

"I'm okay," he said softly.

With a sob, I dropped down and hugged him as hard as I could. "You're okay."

CHAPTER 20

Fake it 'til you make it. Just make it.

We stayed at the lab for over a week. Long enough to bury Barnes (for The Kid's sake, if nothing else) and ensure that the "cure" that had saved David wasn't temporary.

But after lunch on the seventh day, The Kid took us up the elevator and we all stepped into the bright, warm sunlight. Dave and I stared as Robbie motioned toward the same SUV we'd been carried in just a few days later.

"Take it," he said softly. "You earned it."

I spun on The Kid with a gasp. "*Take* it? What do you mean?"

He shrugged. "You can't stay here forever."

Dave nodded as he clutched his still-bandaged hand against his chest. The wound was slow to heal, but it *was* healing.

"That's true, but when we leave you're coming with us."

Robbie looked at us, looked at the SUV, and I could see a big part of him wanted to do just that. But another part, a part that was more man than boy, hesitated.

"There's a lot of dangerous shit in this lab." He smiled as he looked at me. "Sorry, *language*. And there's a lot of good research that can't just be stopped."

I stared at him. "And *you* want to keep that research going?"

He nodded. "Someone has to."

"Honey, you're so young," I whispered. "We can't just leave you here."

The Kid smiled at me, wry and knowing and suddenly *I* felt like the child.

"I-I always knew what he was doing," he said softly.

"You did?" Dave asked in disbelief. "He sort of implied he kept you away from the worst of it."

"He tried, but man, adults are stupid sometimes." Robbie laughed, but his voice cracked. "Even my so-called brilliant dad. He *thought* he was sheltering me, but I hacked into the surveillance camera logs months ago."

"I'm so sorry," I whispered. What The Kid had seen... I couldn't imagine.

He shrugged. "No, *I'm* sorry."

"Why?" Dave asked with a confused shake of his head.

The Kid looked out over the desert.

"I should have stopped him before... I just... I was just too afraid of being alone. That no one would care about me. But then you two came along and I almost got you both killed."

Dave dropped down and looked at Robbie evenly. "If it wasn't for you, I'd be a zombie and Sarah would probably be dead. We owe you *everything*."

The Kid gave a crooked smile. A child and a man all in one. Born in death and undeath.

"Come with us," I pressed.

"Naw," he said, kicking at the dirt. "Somebody's gotta stay and somebody's gotta go."

"Why?" Dave asked.

The Kid dug into his pocket and withdrew something. When he held it out, I reached for it, figuring it was car keys, but instead he plunked a purple vial into my palm.

"Take this. I synthesized it this morning. You'll need it when you head for the Midwest Wall. Maybe the government left over there can use it to re-open the border. Maybe they can work out a way to spread it to all the zombies left."

"What makes you think we're going to the Midwest Wall?" Dave asked as I carefully put the vial in my pocket.

The Kid grinned. "You still want to save the world, right?"

I stared at the precious vial and then I stared at Dave. What The Kid said was right. If we were going to get this thing really distributed, then someone did have to stay and someone had to go. But shit, we couldn't leave him alone, no matter what he said.

"I'll stay," I said softly.

Dave flinched, but he didn't protest, even as he reached out to take my hand.

Robbie was the one who leapt forward. "No! You two are *not* breaking up!"

I blinked to clear the tears from my eyes. "No, but I'm not leaving you alone here, either. So unless you have a better idea…"

There was only silence for a minute, but then The Kid smiled. "Hey, who were those people in the library? The chemist and the girl."

I shook my head, but then I remembered what he was talking about. "Josh and Drea?"

"Yeah, that's them. If he really studied chemistry, he could help me more than you." The Kid chuckled. "Moron."

"Hey!" I said with a laugh, but then I thought about what he had said. Dave and I had figured we might call on Josh and Drea to help us one day. And this one was as good as any. "You're right, though."

"So why not let them in on this shit?" Dave mused. "And they could stay with The Kid while we go to the Wall."

I nodded. It was the best solution. The only solution since the last thing I wanted to do was lose Dave. Again.

Robbie nodded. "As long as they don't treat me like a little kid, I could live with that."

"You *are* a kid," I reminded him, but I ruffled his hair while I did it.

Robbie smiled up at me. "I'll be waiting for them," he said, then he turned and started back into the warehouse. "Better get to it."

We watched him go and waited until we heard the hum of the elevator inside fade away. I stared at David, still stunned by the fact that I'd almost lost him, almost lost everything. But he was whole. Or at least so far.

But we both knew full well we'd just have to wait and see if that was going to change at some point.

"So," I said softly as I reached for his hand. "*Do* we still want to save the world?"

Dave grinned as he opened up the driver's side door and waved me in. He shut it and leaned in through the open window.

"It's about time we did *something*," he said. "And I think world saving has a better health plan than exterminating."

Then he came around to the passenger side and pulled out the GPS. I watched as he entered in Chicago, IL, into the system, our ultimate destination after a quick pit stop to the camp and our friends.

And I put it in gear and we rolled.

ACKNOWLEDGMENTS

I can't say enough good things about the team of publishing professionals who have made creating the "Living with the Dead" series such a wonderful experience. From Jack and Alex in Publicity (who listen to my suggestions and never sigh so I can hear them), to Lauren Panepinto, who designed my kick-ass covers, to Jennifer Flax, who makes the ship go to everyone else who lurks about behind the scenes making my life easier. And then there is Devi Pillai, editor extraordinaire, who talks to me about food on the phone and laughs at my jokes. Awesome.

I also want to acknowledge all the zombie fans who have responded so positively to these stories and shared their excitement (and links to my website) far and wide. I feel like I have my own little zombie posse with you guys around and that's pretty damn cool.

Finally, I have to acknowledge my parents. Daddy, I'm sure if I survived a zombie apocalypse it would be because you taught me everything I needed to know (though I'm sure zombies weren't what you had in mind while teaching me to be a crack shot). And Mom, you have put up with the strangest family possibly in the universe. Thanks for being the "normal" one. Well, normal-ish, anyway.

extras

**SIMON &
SCHUSTER**

London · New York · Sydney · Toronto

A CBS COMPANY

meet the author

A Facebook application once told **Jesse Petersen** that she'd only survive a day in a zombie outbreak, but she doesn't believe that. For one, she's a good shot and two, she has an aversion to bodily fluids, so she'd never go digging around in zombie goo. Until the zombie apocalypse, she lives in the Midwest with her husband and two cats.

Find out more about the author at
www.jessepetersen.net.

introducing

If you enjoyed FLIP THIS ZOMBIE,

look out for

EAT, SLAY, LOVE

Book 3 of Living with the Dead

by Jesse Petersen

Have you ever felt like you were on a treadmill, but no matter how fast or far you ran, you never dropped those pesky last fifteen pounds? Yeah, welcome to my life. Only I'm not trying to lose weight (okay, I'm a girl, I'm *always* trying to lose weight), I'm trying to lose the slobbering, moaning, growling group of mindless zombies that always seems to be on my ass.

Every fucking time I look back over my shoulder, it seems like they are right there. Their feet pound on the pavement, their clawing fingers (complete with long, dirty, dead person fingernails — um, *manicure* people!!) reach for me, trying to give me one scratch, one bite, one little nick that spells certain death...living death...for me.

They never fucking stop. And so *I* never fucking stop. I just run and run and run...

"Sarah?"

With horror movie slowness, I turned and there was David, my husband, my partner in crime and fighting for our lives. He smiled at me, only as his lips pulled back his gums were black. His teeth were beginning to rot. His eyes were red-rimmed and focused on one thing. Eating me.

And not in the porn movie way.

"Stop running," he said, his voice garbled with infection and transition as he reached for me.

I sucked in a breath and sat up, but as I did so my forehead collided with something. Something metal that I smacked into hard enough to make my vision blur.

"Fuck!" I grunted as I reached up to touch my head.

Already the knot of a bruise started to throb just under the skin. Slowly, I opened my eyes and looked around. I willed my heart to slow down. There were no zombies near me. No reaching hands, no frigid breath, no clawing fingers straining to tear and pull at flesh. Just a dim room filled with dusty gym equipment, including the treadmill I had apparently fallen asleep on.

"I *knew* I was on a treadmill," I muttered as I ducked my pounding head from under the bar of the machine and pushed to my feet.

"Did you say something?"

It was David's voice coming from the other room.

Not garbled by infection, though. Just plain old David. I smiled as I moved through the entryway to a weight room. The lack of power made the other equipment in the gym useless except as very uncomfortable beds, but the weight sets still did their job. No juice required.

"Nope, just dreaming," I said. "Nightmaring, I guess, is a better description."

I tilted my head as Dave braced himself on the weight bench and pressed a bar filled with weight plates...a *lot* of weight plates...over his head

"Need a spotter?" I asked as I stepped closer.

"Nope," he grunted. "I got it."

Dave's face was red with strain and sweat rolled down his cheeks to drip on the dusty mat below him. He wasn't wearing a shirt and even more sweat collected on the muscles of his chest. Yeah, you heard me right. My once unemployed, gamer husband with the little beer belly now had ripples of muscle on his chest. He was even starting to get some abs.

Hot.

He held the bar above himself, suspending it as his arms shook ever so slightly. With another grunt, he eased the bar back into place on the rack. Once it was steady, he reached up to wipe the sweat away from his brow with the back of one gloved hand. His gaze came over to me slowly.

"So what was this one about?" he asked as he set his hands back in place and pressed the heavy bar upward again.

This time I counted the weight plates and blinked in surprise. He had to be pushing over 350 pounds. Pretty impressive since I don't think he'd ever topped out over 250 before the zombie outbreak that had changed our lives, and ruined my sleep, forever.

"Sarah?" he asked, his voice strained as he held the bar above his head.

"Huh?" I shook my head. "Oh, just the usual. You know ... getting chased by a horde of drooling zombies."

He lowered the bar again and this time he ducked under and sat up on the bench. He grabbed for a dingy towel that he'd draped across another nearby machine and wiped himself off before he said, "And was I in this one?"

I turned away a little. Dave knew about my dreams. Only because sometimes I talked in my sleep, though. Nothing like screaming out, "Dave, please don't eat me!" to let a guy know you're thinking about him.

"I'll take that as a yes," he said softly. As he peeled off his weight gloves, he pushed to his feet. When he opened his arms, I stepped into them without hesitation. "I'm okay, you know," he whispered after he'd given me a rather sweaty hug for a few minutes.

I nodded, but out of the corner of my eye I looked at his right hand. On it was a scar, black tinged and gnarled, that covered both the top and palm of his hand. It marked the place where a zombie had bitten him over a month ago. If we hadn't had a miracle serum ... a *cure* ... my Dave would have been nothing more than a roaming, mindless eating machine.

Oh, who am I kidding? He would have been a stain on the wall courtesy of yours truly. There's not enough self-help books in the world to get over that one. Trust me, I've looked.

"I know," I whispered as I pulled away with a smile I admit I had to fake. "But you might not have been."

"But I *was*," he insisted with a shake of his head as he patted off his forehead and motioned toward the dressing rooms in the back. I followed close behind.

"I know. And I guess it proved the cure worked. So now we just have to get it to the Midwest Wall."

Dave was silent as he hesitated at the door marked MEN. His frown made my own fake smile fall. Okay, so this rumor about a wall in the Midwest, a way to cut off the zombie infection from the rest of the country...we both knew it was a long shot. But we kept moving toward it. Kept hoping it wasn't all a colossal fake out.

If it was...well, I had no idea what we'd do then. We'd have one vial of a cure and no one to give it to. Plus, since it had taken us a month to get to Oklahoma City, we had to figure it would take us another month to get to the wall, which would put us smack dab in the middle of a Midwest winter, complete with snow, ice, and frigid temps. Fun, eh?

Yeah, sounds like a fucking laugh riot to me.

He motioned me into the dressing room without any more discussion on the touchy subject of walls, or lack thereof. Inside he had set up a portable shower we'd managed to grab from a camping supply store somewhere around Albuquerque. The shower would be cold, but it would do the job. Although since I hadn't actually worked out at the gym we'd taken shelter in, I didn't exactly need it. I was mostly there to stand guard.

Which I did (along with taking a couple of peeks by lamplight at my sweetie soaping up...what? We're married!!). But pretty soon he was changed and we started toward the vestibule of the gym, with Dave loading up a shotgun as we went.

"Okay, so I'd like to get at least thirty miles today," he said as he cocked the shotgun with one hand.

I nodded. So I'm sure that sounds crazy to you. Thirty miles in a day? In the pre-apocalypse days we would have been talking thirty minutes, maybe less. But these are not pre-apocalypse driving conditions, people. There were several things that kept us from getting much farther:

1. We tried to stay off main roads. I mean, big roads meant abandoned cars to move, fires to put out (literally and figuratively), and the occasional highwayman to avoid.
2. We tried to avoid cities. So I'd said we were in Oklahoma City, but that wasn't exactly true. We were actually about fifteen miles north of there in a town called Guthrie. Unlike the real city, which had over five hundred thousand residents who were probably pretty much all zombies now...Guthrie rocked a little less than ten thousand. See what I'm saying?
3. Finally, the last reason we moved so slow became very clear as we stepped up to the floor-to-ceiling glass doors that led to the outside and the parking lot where we'd parked our big old SUV right in a pimp spot.

That reason would be the zombies.

"I guess they saw us come into town," I said mildly as I peered outside. It was early still and the sky was dark from dawn and from the heavy rain clouds that were gathering.

Oh yeah; also it was dark because there was a crowd of about twenty zombies all gathered at the windows, climbing up on top of each other, growling and pawing the glass until they streaked it with sludge and blood and...*goo* of an undefined nature. Which is more disturbing, by the way. Definable goo is way better. Trust me, I'm an expert now.

"I guess they did," Dave said with a long-suffering sigh. He turned toward the check-in desk where we'd left a pile of our shit when we entered the gym last night. There were all kinds of guns in a big mass there, including a super cool multi-shot cannon.

"Well," he said with sigh. "Ready to do this?"

I grabbed two 9mms and slipped clips into place in a smooth motion that had taken months of practice to perfect.

"Fuck yeah. Ready as I'll ever be."

With a half-grin in my direction, Dave flipped the flimsy lock on the glass door and let the horde in.

SIMON &
SCHUSTER

Jesse Petersen

Married with Zombies

The couple who slays together, stays together.

Meet Sarah and David. Sarah and David are like any other couple. They met, they fell in love, but now they're on the verge of divorce. On a routine trip to the marriage counsellor, they notice a few odd things: the lack of cars on the road, the missing security guard, and the fact that their counsellor, Dr Kelly, is ripping out her previous client's throat.

Meet the zombies. Now, Sarah and David are fighting for survival in the middle of the zombie apocalypse. But just because there are zombies, it doesn't mean your other problems go away. And if the zombies don't eat their brains, they might just kill each other.

A romantic comedy with braaaains . . .

ISBN: 978-1-84983-297-7
PRICE £6.99